WELCOME TO THE JUNGLE

WELCOME TO THE JUNGLE

PROTECTED BY THE DAMNED, BOOK 5

MICHAEL TODD   MICHAEL ANDERLE
LAURIE STARKEY

LMBPN

DISRUPTIVE IMAGINATION

Beta Readers

Bree Buras
Dorothy Lloyd
Tom Dickerson
Dorene Johnson
Diane Velasquez

JIT Readers

Tim Bischoff
Kelly O'Donnell
Jim Caplan
Sarah Weir
Peter Manis
Kim Boyer
Kelly Bowerman
John Ashmore
Micky Cocker
Paul Westman
Joshua Ahles

If we missed anyone, please let us know!

Weapons Consultant

John Kern
Proprietor
Spurlock's - Henderson NV

Editor
Lynne Stiegler

DEDICATION

*To Family, Friends and
Those Who Love
to Read.
May We All Enjoy Grace
to Live the Life We Are
Called.*

— Michael Anderle

T'Chezz smashed back into hell, rolling before slamming a fist on the ground. His hands clenched and his legs trembled. Slowly he stood up, growling, his teeth dripping saliva.

The ground shook as the portal closed and he was left right back where he had started, only this time with a gift.

He cursed and grabbed the car with both hands, crushing it into a ball, then yelled in anger and slammed it to the ground like a basketball. This ball didn't bounce, though. Instead, shards of twisted metal bounced off and rattled across the ground.

T'Chezz let out a deep breath and stomped around for a few moments, finally grabbing the hunk of metal and bitching as he moved toward his castle. He issued commands to the sycophants on his way in. When he entered his office, he walked over to a corner and tossed the new artwork on the floor.

In fact, T'Chezz had expensive taste, always lifting

something historical or precious before returning to hell. Last time it was Michelangelo's "Leda and the Swan," which Italians were still searching for last time he had gone aboveground, and Johannes Vermeer's "The Concert" which he had read was thought to have been stolen.

Either way, that ball of metal was the most important thing on his mind at that moment. He picked the car up, set it on the pedestal, and stood back to stare at it, seething in anger at the fact that he hadn't even set foot onto that desert before being sent back down. He couldn't just stand by; he knew that things were going to get complicated if he didn't get control of these damn demon hunters. He needed someone on the inside; someone who could give him details and knowledge of where these hunters were and how to destroy them.

He had been on Earth often enough to know that the human conscience was flexible, so there would definitely be someone in the Damned willing to do a deal with him.

There always was.

"Your Grace," one of the sniveling servants said, bowing. "You requested the one who calls himself 'the Ivy.'"

"Stupid name," T'Chezz growled under his breath. "Yes. Is he here?"

"Yes." He bowed and opened the door.

One of the more powerful demons entered. His walk was more human-like than the normal scuttling most demons did. He bowed his head to T'Chezz and took a seat. The demon leader walked over to the window and ran his hand across the weapons sitting on the table underneath it. He was tired of losing, and at this point he would try anything to get to the Killers.

"I have a job for you," T'Chezz growled quietly. "You owe me a favor, so I figure this is the perfect time. I need you to go to Earth, find a host, and infiltrate the Damned. I need one of them to make a deal with me; give up the whereabouts of the Killers and their toys. That team is the only thing standing in the way of my taking over. I am choosing *you* for this because, though you are boring as hell, you always get the job done."

"I'm fastidious and driven," the demon replied. "I am not *mischievous*. It is a downfall of so many of our kind and humans, T'Chezz. It is why our kind have problems, and why humans suffer our advances."

"Uh huh." T'Chezz rolled his eyes. "Report back when you've gotten me something."

The demon nodded, got up from the chair, and walked out of the room. T'Chezz's servant went to close the door, but he stopped him.

"Do something for me," T'Chezz requested, rubbing his chin.

"Yes, sir," he replied.

"I want you to speak with Zallot for me. Make sure that asshole Ivy is taken care of when he is finished," T'Chezz told him, rubbing his hands together. "His usefulness to me is at an end. I won't miss him for a few hundred years."

"I will make sure it is done, and report back as soon as he has completed the task, sir," the servant replied, nodding.

"Good." T'Chezz laughed evilly. "And leave the car there for now. It's a nice addition, don't you think?"

"Very nice, sir," the demon agreed fearfully.

"Right." T'Chezz looked at the servant with distaste. "That will be all."

He walked to the window again, this time feeling a lot better about his plans. The one thing that has always been true was that humans could be bought with the promise of a good life…and this was the perfect opportunity to exploit that.

He was going to get Korbin's Killers and bring his sister back down to hell, squashing her little human in the process.

No one hit T'Chezz with a car and lived to tell about it.

Korbin, Calvin, Katie, and Damian sat around the large table in the conference room, staring at each other. There was a lot to talk about between the move, the changes in Katie with Pandora, and the fact that they weren't going to be able to keep the weapons hidden much longer.

Katie hated when they had to talk about her abilities, but it was a conversation that needed to be had so everyone was on the same page. Korbin shuffled through the report of the last fight and took off his thin-rimmed reading glasses, tossing them on the papers and leaning back.

"So, how about it?" Calvin asked. "Do you think it's time to come clean about Katie and Pandora with the others? Are they ready to accept something like that?"

"My first instinct is to be honest," Korbin said. "But I fear that in this case honesty will ultimately lead to an inability for me to protect Katie to my full ability. When you see her in action you get it, but when it's explained it seems a lot dicier. And none of them know her like we do."

"I'm right here," Katie reminded him.

"I know," Korbin replied. "I'm sorry, I'm not used to having this conversation *with* you instead of *about* you."

"Well, if it's any consolation, I agree with you," Katie told him. "I don't know if the other teams can handle a change like that. *We* barely handle it on a daily basis. If *you* questioned it at the beginning, then you know they will, hands down."

"You're right." Korbin sighed.

"I can agree on that," Calvin interjected. "Damian? What do you think?"

"I have to agree," he began carefully. "I saw the struggle Korbin went through when it all began, and what kept him straight is the fact that he knows Katie. The fact that he cares for her as part of this team. Without that, though?" He paused for a moment. "I'm not sure they would even try to understand. Fear can be a powerful thing, and people tend to fear what they don't understand."

"All right," Korbin agreed. "The other team leads are coming to the base. Well, whatever is left of it, anyway. We are going to have a confab over the weapons. It's time they got theirs, and are made aware of the importance of keeping them secret. Katie, I want you to go out of town for a day or two, just so things don't get dicey. I know what will happen: we will get a call while they are here. I don't want them finding out in the heat of battle, since they'd likely strike you down without thinking about it."

"I know!" Damian offered, sitting up. "I'll take her to

Disneyland. Buy some mouse ears, ride the Teacups, get some good food."

"I don't know about Disneyland," Korbin said doubtfully. "I would stick to somewhere like Los Angeles. At least there she is less likely to be spotted as a demon since it's…well, Hollywood, to be honest."

Hey! Pandora exclaimed in Katie's mind. *I resemble that remark.*

Katie pressed her lips together and looked down, trying not to smirk at Pandora's comment. She was finding it harder and harder to not let it be known that her demon was talking to her. Pandora had become kind of an everyday thing for her by this point.

"I will let the LAPD know that the two of you are coming into town," he continued. "After you guys kicked ass last time, they started requesting that we let them know when you are in town in case we are looking for something they can help with, or if they need an extra set of hands. It will also keep them from panicking that there is about to be an incursion."

"Sounds good." Katie smiled.

"We can go to Universal Studios," Damian suggested. "It's close enough to Hollywood that no one will pay attention to your beady red eyes."

"Hey, I'm not the only one with red rings, my friend." Katie smirked.

"True." Damian stood up. "Is that all for now, Korbin?"

"Yep. Just be safe."

"We would be safer if I had my damn car," Katie grumbled as she collected her things. "Seriously, I hope my license plate is imprinted on T'Chezz's balls. It would fucking serve him right."

"If it's any help, we all thank you for your sacrifice." Calvin chuckled. "We know how much that car meant to you."

"It *isn't* any help." Katie shook her head. "The things I do for my country!"

Korbin snickered. "A proud patriot."

"One day you will lose something precious, and I don't want you coming to me complaining," Katie warned them, sticking out her tongue. "It was my pride and joy."

"And you are ours." Damian bowed as the two walked toward the door. "Like a shining beacon of hope."

Katie snorted. "Right."

Stephanie stood in the doorway of the conference room as Katie and Damian walked toward her. She had rushed from the house, having done some last-minute things to help the girls get packed up, and was running late. She knew Korbin was rarely on time for meetings anyway, so she had just tried to get there *somewhat* promptly.

"Am I interrupting?" Stephanie asked.

"Nope," Katie replied, giving her a high-five. "Just discussing my car."

"Still?" Stephanie chuckled.

"She is only in the second stage of mourning," Damian replied with a smirk.

"Hey, that thing was like part of my body." Katie pouted as she walked out of the office and down the hall.

Damian laughed and followed her, leaving Stephanie to join Calvin and Korbin at the big round table. Korbin smiled at her as she walked in. She was wearing jeans and a tank top with her pink Chuck Taylors. She had dived head-first back into being the woman she wanted to be, not the one she'd had to pretend to be.

"Howdy!" She sat down at the table. "What's up?"

"I'd like you to tell me more about your land," Korbin replied.

"Well, it's plenty of space…over a hundred acres," she began. "I am assuming you are going to build a base on it?"

"Yeah, that's the plan. We have to get out of here as soon as possible, though," he replied.

"That shouldn't be an issue," she said. "There is an old ICBM facility on the land that, with a little love and care, you could stay in while you build your new base."

Calvin chuckled. "Did they leave any presents behind?"

"Yeah, a bunch of dust and trash," she answered. "But you could build your base around it. Probably incorporate part of it into the new digs."

"Good," Korbin replied. "I have to admit, my first effort at finding anything—especially in our territory—has been a complete and utter failure. It's either too close to civiliza-tion, for commercial only use, or it's wayyyy overpriced. I need something that I can eventually build an airfield on, and I have found absolutely nothing."

"Well, you could do that on my land, but until that comes about, there are other options," she told him. "I suggest you invest in a helicopter instead of renting. You can either chopper to the location, or if it's a longer trip, right to the airport. It will save time fighting traffic, and helicopters can now carry a hell of a lot of stuff. I mean seriously, it's not like there aren't a million choppers flying around Vegas at any given time. You will blend right in; no one will even know the difference."

"I like that…all of that," Korbin admitted, rubbing his chin. "I agree, we *do* need our own helicopter. It would make things a hell of a lot more efficient. That kind of money will have to be okayed by the higher-ups, but I am pretty sure they will be more than happy to send one over since we have been doing well."

"You mean *Katie* has." Stephanie chuckled.

"With the big ones, yeah, but whatever pays the bills." Korbin laughed and opened his laptop. "I just want to see how close your land is to Area 51."

He pulled up the map and put in the address, then leaned back and stared at the screen. He could see that the two places were fairly far apart and he nodded, then looked at Stephanie's land from every direction. He had to be sure. He couldn't build something like the facility he was thinking if anyone in the government might catch on.

"It actually looks to be a perfect distance away from Area 51," he mused. "But let me ask you this: why do you still have that land? You are Damned, and I am pretty sure you were put into the system as deceased. I really don't want the government to come looking for the land or the owner."

"They won't," she assured him. "I bought the property under the radar from someone who needed to get out of a dire situation. I put it under my mother's maiden name, and I paid for it in cash. As far as they know someone else owns it, and unless we give them reason, they aren't going to come scratching around."

He got down to brass tacks. "Okay, so how much for us to occupy the space?"

"Well, I won't sell it, but you guys can stay there for free," she started. "I guess 'you guys' includes me. However, I have one stipulation: if you ever leave, I get to keep the upgrades at no cost."

"Wow." He laughed. "That's a tall order. How about you keep the upgrades at ten percent of the cost or $1,500,000, whichever is cheaper."

"You will be living on the land for free," she argued.

"Yeah, but the land is not even *close* to being worth the same amount as the structures I will be building on it."

"Five percent," Stephanie negotiated.

"Ten," Korbin replied. "Not budging."

"Ugh." She rolled her eyes. "Fine, ten percent."

"Good." He smiled. "Let's get this show on the road, then."

"Yeah, whatever," Stephanie grumbled quietly as she got up from the table. "You are *such* an obstinate sonofabitch."

Damian and Katie left the house through the front door rather than the garage entryway for the first time in a long time, taking their luggage with them for the trip.

The garage wasn't really a safe area, so they had parked the SUVs elsewhere. Damian took Katie's bags from her and loaded them into one of the black SUVs. When he came around to the driver's side to get in, she was still standing where he had left her and staring at the compound.

Even Damian had to admit that the place was a complete and total disaster area. It looked like a tornado had gone through, destroying everything in its path—and she knew that part of that was because of her. Even though she had fought the demon off and helped save everyone, her home lay in ruins.

Damian reached up and squeezed her shoulder. She sighed and got into the SUV, turning her eyes away.

It could have been much worse, but still, lives had been lost and a home had been destroyed. It was terrible that it had happened, but she had to come to terms with it. She didn't need that added stress.

On one hand she was glad that she was getting away for a day or so. On the other hand, she didn't want to have to hide from the world because except for her team, her family—the rest of the teams, the people who were supposed to be there for her—were too caught up in past experiences to accept that she could help.

Once again, she felt as if she were alone on an island because of her demon.

"Do you think the demons will come back?" Damian asked, putting the car in drive.

Katie wanted so badly to tell him that it was all over—that the demons had given up—but she knew that wasn't the truth.

Sure, the demons wouldn't be coming back to the base, but that didn't mean that everything was in the clear. There was still a lot going on behind the scenes; there was a worldwide demon infestation, and it was only going to get worse.

The best thing she could do at that point was be honest, but not so honest that it freaked him out.

"It's unlikely," Katie replied. "Pandora says that something of that magnitude and effort probably cost T'Chezz a lot of power. Pandora is pretty sure he decided to invade the compound on very short notice. Apparently he doesn't have much self-control when it comes to revenge or anger, and though he makes plans, he tends to deviate from them when he gets emotional. On top of that, he is attacking all over the world. This isn't a single effort. He's just obsessed with us—for personal reasons most likely."

"Great, an emotional demon." Damian laughed.

He has no freaking clue. Pandora scoffed. *You think I'm bad? Just wait for that ball of emotional bullshit. Seriously, he is like a human girl with the worst PMS you have ever seen. I knew as soon as I felt yours that I had to stop that crazy shit.*

I was wondering why I haven't been visited by Aunt Flo since I met you. Katie sighed.

"Are there other major demons involved in all this?" Damian asked, having no idea what Katie and Pandora were talking about.

"They all have their own plans in place, I'm sure," Katie told him. "If it looks like he is getting close to world domination, he will have to deal with the guys above him. T'Chezz will make it a point to be on this side before that happens, though. In hell they can easily overcome him, but if he's here they are less likely to try to take him and more likely to negotiate."

"Gotcha," Damian replied uneasily, driving through the city toward the highway. "I guess we need to be prepared for anything, then."

"That's the best tack," Katie replied, watching out the window.

They drove in silence for quite a while, Katie thinking about the whole situation. It was a difficult one, rife with politics and questions. The politics, though—they were different than the ones she would normally see. Even Katie didn't fully grasp the depth of them.

She tapped a finger to the beat of the music in the car as they drove down the 15 toward LA. She wanted so badly for it to be over. To have the chance to feel like a person again. At this point she was starting to feel like a prisoner, only her captor really wasn't that hard to get along with—and she kept her skinny with tits aimed high into the sky, defying gravity.

She guessed it could be worse. She could have gotten an asshole demon with irritatingly bad breath or something.

"You hungry?" Damian asked. "You can tell Pandora there is a donut shop ahead."

Nope, Pandora growled. *Don't want any.*

Why? Katie replied with a chuckle. *I thought donuts were your favorite.*

You tricked me with those potato-based ones. They were so bad you killed it for me, she snarled. *I'm still trying to decide whether you did that on purpose.*

Katie chuckled, which forced Damian to look at her, waiting to hear what she was laughing about. The truth was, she actually hadn't done it on purpose. She had just been trying to get her to taste new things, but it had seemed to work out for the better—Katie's better.

She was starting to think that if Pandora ever left her body she was destined for diabetes and obesity, with all kinds of addictions to sugar and fatty foods. She was very glad she hadn't introduced the demon to soda yet. Katie looked at him and shook her head.

"What?" Damian exclaimed in surprise. "I thought Pandora was a glutton for donut heaven."

Katie laughed. "She had a terrible experience with a potato donut recently. *I* thought they were good, but there are still two of them left at home. I guess she didn't have the same feelings as me, not to mention they are not very good when you warm them up."

Damn right, Pandora grumbled. *You did that shit on purpose, I know it. What's next—bad Italian?*

Whoa, Katie replied. *Now, I can be devious and everything, but you are taking this too far. I would never mess with the Italian, and besides, I have to put it in my body.*

Yeah, well, I don't trust you anymore, not as far as I can throw you, Pandora told her. *I guess that's a bad analogy, I can probably throw you pretty fucking far, even from in here.*

Let's not test that theory, Katie shot back.

"You need to get that demon some good donuts." Damian shook his head. "She needs to try Krispy Kreme. Not only do they make them fresh so you can buy them hot, but they also microwave well in about twelve seconds. It's the king of donuts, especially for people who take them home with them."

Pandora sniffed. *Maybe.*

"She said she will think about it," Katie shared.

A vehicle pulled up outside; a blacked-out SUV, new and shiny, chauffeuring the heads of the teams to the compound for an eye-opening demonstration of the power of their new weapons.

None of them knew why they were there, though. They assumed they would discuss the destruction of the base, and the future of the demons. Korbin looked out the window as they piled out of the SUV and were greeted by Calvin. They all looked horrified; completely shocked at how badly the place had been torn up. William Hunt, Amy Brown, and Brian Hudson had all come, as had John William Smith from New York.

Korbin took a deep breath and made his way to the main living quarters to meet the team leads. He wanted to give them a tour first; let them know what happened, rather than take them straight to the weapons. When he got up to the area Calvin was talking casually with them, making them laugh as he always did. He was a good person to have as a second. He always put people at ease with his laid-back personality and calm demeanor.

Amy walked over to him and looked around before sticking out her hand. "Korbin, I'm so sorry for all this. It looks like you guys got hit hard. Fortunately you still have living quarters, but damn! It looks like everything else is shot."

"Thank you." Korbin nodded, and thought about it again. "Yeah, we didn't fare too well, but most of us are still standing and that's what matters."

"Korbin, it's good to see you." John nodded and reached out to shake Korbin's hand. "It's been a long time. I'm here representing the majority of the East Coast, since the others couldn't make it."

"Glad to have you, John," Korbin replied. "All of you, for that matter. Let's take a little tour while I explain more about how this attack happened."

Korbin showed the team leaders through the compound, careful not to let them near the business side of things. They looked at the downed buildings from a distance, making the excuse that they were too dangerous to enter. He talked as they walked, giving them the general outline of the whole ordeal.

"A large and dangerous demon we have come to know as 'T'Chezz' opened a portal along the road leading to the compound," Korbin explained. "He was stopped from coming through when Katie ran a car into him, knocking him back through the portal and closing it. Luckily, she wasn't injured. However, dozens of demons had come through before we were able to shut it and they all ran at the compound, ready to fight. They were like an army."

"We saw the tire tracks leaving the road and heading out through the sand as we were driving in," Brian explained. "We just thought someone was playing around out there."

"No, those were from the car she used to ram the demon." He shrugged. "Right time and right place, I suppose."

"And you all battled these demons?" William asked.

"Yes," Korbin confirmed, leaving out the girls and Stephanie. "We headed some off outside, but when they broke through we battled them inside—which is where all the damage came from."

"How big were they?" Amy asked.

"There were several large demons, but the rest were normal ones," Korbin replied. "The big ones were taken down by the team, except for one which was eaten by another to gain power."

"That's...*interesting*." Amy reviewed her memories. "Haven't seen that before."

"Neither had we," Korbin admitted, stopping and turning to them. "In the last moments of the battle the demon raged, blowing through the other buildings. It took Katie, Damian, and Eric to finally put the beast down."

"I don't mean to question you," John asked, "but a demon that size and three normal hunters? That sounds like it would be an awful lot for them to handle."

"I would agree, but I heard about Los Angeles." Amy shrugged. "Still, there had to be something else involved with all this. Maybe some special somethings you aren't telling us?"

Korbin shuffled his feet as he looked at each of their faces. He had known it wouldn't be that easy to fool them, but he wasn't prepared to tell them about Katie yet. They had agreed that would be a bad idea, and he was going to stick to that decision.

"Actually," Korbin continued, "that's why I brought you here. I *do* have a secret, but I think that it may be a bit different than what you are thinking. There are no super-powers or a Hulk waiting in the wings."

"Then what is it?" Amy asked.

"Weapons," Korbin told them. "And not just any weapons, very special ones. Follow me, and I will show you. And by the way, where are your seconds?"

"Oh, we all left them back in charge at the bases," William explained. "We knew you had been attacked, and we didn't want to leave our people completely unprotected with that kind of threat out there."

"Got it." Korbin nodded. "Good decisions."

"So, we heard you picked up a new Damned," Brian said. He was walking next to Korbin. "Another female, younger than you but older than the others. How is she?"

"Her name is Stephanie," Korbin replied. "And she is

good. She is trained in martial arts, strong, mentally capable, and very loyal. I tried to get her to go to one of you, but she insisted on staying with us."

"What kind of demon?" John asked.

"A succubus." Korbin blushed slightly. "She owned a brothel before becoming one of the Damned. I guess that was where she got the demon."

"That should be interesting." Amy laughed. "With all these men in here."

"She isn't like that," Korbin replied. "She is very respectable, and controls her demon really well. She actually has been quite helpful recently, donating some land for us to build our new base on."

"I was going to ask you if you planned on staying," Brian replied. "Though this would take a major rebuild."

"Yeah." Korbin shook his head. "I thought about rebuilding here, but our cover is blown, and I can't keep the civilian authorities away for too long if they continue to try to attack us. I figured it was time to move on to the next place."

"Good thinking," Amy agreed. "Are there facilities there?"

"An old base for us to stay in initially," Korbin replied, pressing the elevator button. "But I plan on building a whole new base around it."

"And what did the higher-ups say?" William asked.

"Are you kidding?" Brian laughed. "This team is on fire! The higher-ups will probably give him anything he needs."

"True." Korbin chuckled. "But I am building the base myself, or at least most of it. I made a deal with Stephanie."

Korbin stopped in front of the conference room and

the elevator doors shut behind him. He looked at each of the leaders in turn, just to make sure that they were on the same side as him. He smiled at Amy, who knew exactly what he was doing.

Korbin smiled. "The surprise is through here, but I need to know that I have your discretion. That you won't speak of what you are about to see, even with the government."

"What do you have back there?" Amy chuckled, trying to look over his shoulders.

"Godzilla." Brian laughed. "You have my discretion."

"And mine," Amy replied.

"Always," William assured him.

"John?" Korbin asked, turning to him.

"Well, I don't know you as well as the others, but curiosity has me on pins and needles, so you have mine too," John assured him.

"All right, then let's get this over with," Korbin replied.

The demon had situated his things just perfectly, knowing he would be gone for a bit. He didn't want to leave a mess. He was not a normal demon, but rather was purposeful about everything he did. He left the underworld and traveled up, searching for a "proper" human to take over.

The capsule not only had to suit his style—be neat, tidy, and pay close attention to detail—but it also had to be someone who could get close to the Damned; talk to one of them about the betrayal.

The demon ended up in New York, a city he loved for the excitement but hated due to the lack of order and the resulting chaos.

He needed order. He needed everything to be in its place, he planned things out, and he allowed no spontaneity. That was just how he was, even though his instincts were quite the opposite.

Finally, after days of searching and then a day or two of

stalking and planning, the neat-freak demon found a Coven whose leader, Bridgett, had yet to be infected.

She *wanted* to be infected. In fact, she prayed for it and thought about it constantly, and the stench of jealousy on her when she was around the Damned in her coven was more than disgusting to the demon. He didn't want to be cooped up inside a human, but he knew that to have even a chance of getting close to the Damned he *needed* her.

After several days of watching, the demon took her while she was asleep. He had found that way to be the most effective, since he could keep the human from passing out or vomiting during the experience, due to his power.

Bridgett woke up afterward. "Oh damn!" She slid out bed and moved to her dresser.

"*Yes!*" Her eyes were red and she could feel something inside, but he wasn't moving or talking.

This was not how she had heard it usually happened.

Hello? she called mentally. *Anyone in here? Can you talk back?*

Obviously I'm in here, a voiced snapped derisively. *But until I have orders for you, I will remain quiet.*

Her brows narrowed. *I thought I was supposed to be the leader here.*

Yeah, you keep thinking that. He scoffed. *Anyway, brush that hair, put on some clothes and go about your day.*

"Whatever," she grumbled out loud, then she felt the unyielding need to follow his instructions.

The demon wasn't going to take her shit, and being one of the more powerful ones, he set himself up to control as many of her actions as he could without completely giving her away.

The last thing he wanted—or needed, for that matter—was to be tracked down by the Killers before he'd had a chance to speak to one of them. Until that point, he would keep Bridgett on a short leash. It was always better to be the one in control.

He didn't mind this human as much as the last he'd had to deal with. She was well groomed, got up on time, spoke fluently and intelligently, and generally didn't make him want to puke. But still, she wasn't up to par with what he deserved.

This was a short-notice gig, which was just like T'Chezz, but he owed him a favor, so there he was.

Next time he would think it through before he asked anyone like T'Chezz for a favor. Missions like these were not his favorite things, but then again, rotting in hell was not very exciting either.

He put on a brave demon face and decided to make the most of it. At least Earth had good food, and better conversation than he had been having with the idiots below.

No matter *how* strong they were. Strength did *not* equate with intelligence.

When the human had cleaned up and made herself as pretty as she could, the demon directed her to go about her day. There was no time to lose, especially not on human bullshit.

Bridgett went out to a restaurant and sat—back straight as a statue's—at an outside table, staring down at the menu.

The demon read it over and sighed, not impressed by her choice of restaurant. He made a mental note to make her do some research next time before taking him out to a place to eat. He didn't need food to survive, but *she* did, so he picked the most appetizing thing—to him—on the menu.

Order two eggs, sunny-side up, an English muffin, lightly toasted, and a hot cup of coffee, he told her.

She did so and then sat there in a light trance, folding her napkin neatly in her lap and placing her hands on top. The waitress looked at her strangely, but shrugged and kept going. Bridgett stared at the table as she waited for the demon to speak. She had wanted this for so long, but it didn't seem to be anything like she thought a possession would be.

I am here looking for the Damned. The Killers, to be precise, the demon told her. *I need someone who may be willing to strike a deal.*

Someone to make a deal with the Devil? she clarified, surprised.

Precisely, he agreed. *Have you heard of them? They haven't been so quiet recently with their attempts to take down the demon race.*

I know of them, she qualified, thinking this through. *I try to stay away from them for safety reasons. I've known one of them for a while.*

A coven head and a Damned know each other, the demon mused. *Interesting. Go on.*

He doesn't know that I'm in a coven. If he ever found out, I would be dead in a heartbeat. I know him, he knows me, but we aren't more than passing acquaintances. For good reasons, I have kept him at arm's length.

No matter. You know who he is, he knows who you are—that is perfect, the demon snarled.

She thought about their options. *I also know he hates to*

be anything less than Number One. He is constantly racing toward the future, trying to get ahead. Sometimes he seems almost obsessed with the idea of perfection.

He sounds like the perfect candidate, the demon replied, wondering why he never got those kinds of humans to possess.

I bet he would like to know what you are offering, Bridgett said. *And maybe we can get him to see the opportunity as a positive thing. It's important to keep him or speak to him away from the others, though. Something secretive will grab his attention. I will have to be quick, though. He will know I am infected the moment he sees my eyes, and I really would like to keep my head on my shoulders.*

The demon waited a minute before speaking again. *Hmmm. You may be right. Maybe you will be more useful than I originally had considered.* She perked up a touch with his compliment. *I am sure I can protect you from whatever you are afraid of, which in this case seems to be death. Humans are so interesting; so curious, when it comes to things like that. Death should be the least of your worries. This world is full of despicable and disgusting people. I know, because I used to frequent their bodies.*

Bridgett opened her mouth to say something, but he didn't feel like hearing her philosophy on death so he cut her short.

She closed her mouth and pouted. He controlled the way she moved her mouth. She must have looked insane sitting there fighting to get her mouth open; fighting to do anything other than stare. Finally the waitress came back with her food, and smiled down at her. She forced a smile in return and picked up her coffee.

Bridgett sighed. *Okay, I'll be quiet. Jesus!*

Eat your breakfast. We have a plan to hatch, and for fuck's sake—never say that name!

Korbin looked at each team lead to make sure that their faces were resolute.

He hated questioning his own family but these days he had to be more careful than usual.

Many people had been betrayed in the previous year, so he was making damn sure he and his team wouldn't become the next victims.

These were the most upstanding leaders of the teams, and he would need their help keeping the weaponry a secret from the government. The smaller teams would get the new weapons too, but the main hubs were his focus. It was vital that they be brought in before they started to ask more questions.

He unlocked the door and led them across the room to the massive metal safe against the back wall. It looked like the old-time vaults; the ones that had rolled to be into banks before they built the secure rooms.

However, this one's door was completely up to date on all security protocols.

He pushed in the code to the finger pad, pressed his thumb to the scanner, leaned down for an eye scan, and when it clicked, turned the knob, opening the door wide to reveal the weapons the company created for them.

They shimmered and sparkled in their display case, and Korbin could almost feel the power radiating through them. There were twelve weapons, enough for each team lead to take home three. The team leads gaped at the bright weapons. They weren't sure what was so special about them, but they too could feel the otherworldly presence pulsing from their long, sharp blades.

"Who is going to be tested first?" Korbin asked with a straight face.

The leads looked at him, and then each other. They had no idea what he meant by "tested first," and they couldn't seem to keep their eyes off the weapons.

Korbin smirked as he stared at the four of them, his arms crossed over his chest. After several moments of silence Amy stepped forward, rolling her eyes and throwing her hands in the air.

Korbin had figured she would probably go first, since she was the bravest of them all. She was small and had just a small touch of the Napoleon complex, but she had been his favorite of the leaders for a long time.

"Bunch of rabbits," she grumbled, looking at the men in annoyance as she stepped forward. "Korbin isn't going to hurt us."

She shook her head as Korbin took her hand and grabbed a small knife from the vault. Before she could even look back at Korbin, he pricked the tip of her finger and let go.

She looked at him strangely for a fraction of a moment before pulling her hand up to her chest, her eyes opening wide in surprise. Sweat beaded on her forehead and her face went pale as she worked to stop any noise from escaping her lips.

Her eyes declared their intent to plug Korbin full of laser holes if she could just shoot them from those orbs.

"*FUUUUCK!*," she finally groaned. "What the *holy* hell did you just do to me? Goddamn, it feels like fucking *fire!*"

She put her finger into her mouth and closed her eyes. Korbin could remember how strong that feeling had been when he was pricked for the first time. He had kept his composure better than Amy, though.

When the pain subsided, she hopped back to the others and pushed John forward.

"You're up!" She looked at John, her lips smiling but her eyes promising pain.

"Great." John stepped forward. "Just what I was looking forward to this morning—a stabbing."

One by one the leaders stepped up to the front, allowing Korbin to prick their fingers. All four of them had a bad reaction, cursing and growling at the full effect of the knives.

They were not happy to have been wounded like that, but it had definitely intrigued them.

"What is this?" John asked. "Where did you find it?"

"Well, we met a young man at a weapons fair we attended," Korbin explained. "He'd inherited a centuries-old skill, and it was the breakthrough we needed. We knew as soon as the metal was near us that it was something special. I am a minority owner in the company, Katie being the main stockholder, and a few others taking board seats with small shares of the company. The young man originally running it was orphaned at a young age and was living in his van. He was traveling around making these weapons, but never really selling them. It is a very well-hidden centuries-old secret, used long ago to defeat an incursion of demons and now in our hands. We felt we needed to move on it quickly."

"I would tend to agree," Amy exclaimed, examining a sword "This might have something to do with why the demons attacked the base. These would not go over well in the demon community. I suppose these are what you used when you were defeating those guys?"

"It was, and I agree," Korbin told her. "Our team heavy found him tucked away at the event, bought the company right there, and brought him back with us. It's just him, so it took a while to build up enough of a supply to give you guys some. It was a spur-of-the-moment decision that has since saved our lives more than once."

"I would like to meet your team heavy," John said, looking at the sword. "She seems to have an eye for weaponry."

"And everything else." Amy scoffed. "She is the one who created our team-wide creed. She was apparently small and quiet at first, but I've heard she is definitely on warrior status now."

"She is quite the Killer." Korbin chuckled. "She was found in an abandoned parking garage, tied to a pole and newly infected. I didn't have high hopes for her longevity, but she has become one of my best fighters—though sometimes she can get carried away."

"It seems it pays off, though," Amy countered. "Those demons she kills are pretty hefty."

"That they are. She wanted to meet you as well, but unfortunately she couldn't be here for this meeting," Korbin said. "Next time we get together, she will be there."

"Good," John exclaimed.

John was experienced, more because of the sheer number of demons that hit the New York area than the years under his belt.

Korbin had never really liked him that much. He was pushy and competitive, and out of all the team leads he was the *last* one that he would trust with Katie's secret.

He couldn't be sure John wouldn't have her transferred to his team by the higher-ups—or even worse, be the one to drive a sword through her heart.

Now that everyone was there with Korbin, he had started to realize just how important it was to keep her abilities a secret. Much like the swords, she was a precious weapon; poised and ready for battle, never letting the team down.

Her safety had just become his primary focus. Unfortunately, needs must when the Devil drove.

4

The car slowly came to a stop in front of the fancy hotel Damian had booked for them. It went up eight stories, the grey stone etched by history even as a fresh coat of paint tried to liven it up a touch.

They went inside, checked in, and put their stuff in their rooms. As usual they had adjoining rooms, since Damian was constantly worried that Katie would be attacked.

He was the only one who knew T'Chezz was Pandora's brother, and he was aware of the animosity between the two.

Katie was between the fighting siblings.

Their rooms were huge, with sleek eclectic furniture, huge jetted tubs, marble everywhere, and comfortable, inviting beds. It was tempting to stay in and sleep their mini-vacation away, and Katie mentioned that fact.

Damian sighed. "That's not going to happen."

Katie was excited to be a tourist for a little while in the

city, especially since the last time she had been there with Calvin the two of them nearly died. She wanted to walk around the town like a normal person, taking pictures at Grauman's Chinese Theatre, walking on the stars, and shaking Spiderman's hand. She knew it was stupid, but she wasn't about to let something like that pass her by.

She was not used to seeing other places, and she wanted to take full advantage of it while she could.

When everything was put away in their rooms, Katie met Damian in the hall so they could explore Hollywood.

She was as excited as if it were Christmas morning. Damian just laughed and shook his head.

"All right!" She grinned. "We can go on a tour of the stars' homes, eat amazing sushi, take a picture of the Hollywood sign, and get an autograph from someone famous. My list went goes on and on!"

And not one spa day here?

Trust me. Katie snickered. *Even* you *wouldn't like spa days in this area.*

Why? All gay men?

No, very little food, and what food they have is nasty. Nothing but pain in order to force you to look pretty by taking away anything you might enjoy.

What are these people, assholes? Pandora asked.

Well, the rumor is if they weren't before they start their spa day, they are by the end. Then, the next day they brag to their friends like they just raced in the Iditarod in Alaska. Then that friend goes through hell...oh.

She wasn't sure she would have enough time there to get through her list, but she was hell-bent on giving it a try.

"So, what do you want for lunch?" Damian asked. "Donuts?"

"She isn't asking for donuts, oddly enough," Katie told him. "I thought it was just her being stubborn at first over the potato ones."

"That's a good thing, though, right?" Damian asked as they made their way through the hotel and outside past the hotel's doorman.

"You would think," Katie replied absently as she looked both left and right before heading left. "But silence usually means something else is up. I just don't know what it is…yet."

"Maybe she is just being nice," Damian suggested with a smile.

"Yeah, right." She scoffed.

BWAHAHAHAHAHAHA, *silly priest.* Pandora stopped. *Oooh, look, the stars!*

Katie looked down at the stars as they walked over them. There were many of them; some she recognized, and some she didn't. She wondered what the appeal of having your name on a star was, but then she was not fond of being the center of attention.

That was one of the few reasons she didn't like volley-ball; when you made a good play or saved the game, everyone wanted to pat you on the back.

It had occasionally made her want to hide.

Hmm, Desi Arnaz. Pandora pointed out. *From* I Love Lucy. *He had a serious obsession with Lucy. He used to chase her around wearing her robe and slippers, singing at the top of his lungs. It was a big scandal, but they covered it up.*

Uhm, I don't think... Katie stopped as Pandora started again.

Oh, Eve Arden! What a dear. Pandora sighed. *She was fabulous in everything she did, but she seriously hated the bigger stars. She was tired of getting supporting actress awards. I heard that she only won the best actress because she threatened the lives of everyone on the board for the Oscars. She had a real serious dark side to her. I am pretty sure she went to my house when she died. And here—the famous Joan Collins, who, by the way, has a seriously loud and obnoxious demon inside her.*

As much as I want to admit that may be true for Joan Collins, I am pretty sure you just made the rest of that shit up. Katie chuckled. *Though the vision of Desi Arnaz in Lucy's robe is pretty entertaining.*

Fine, Pandora grumped. *So I lied. Whatever. What does it matter? They are stupid star-shaped stones on the ground. My stories were funny, weren't they? And probably a hell of a lot more entertaining than their real stick-in-the-mud lives anyway.* She paused for a moment. *If I was lying.*

You are too much. Katie laughed. *Maybe you should write my eulogy when I die. I will either be a psycho, or the most amazing woman who ever lived. Either way, it will be entertaining.*

I would, but when you die I am back in my hellhole...or worse, Pandora griped.

Oh, yeah. Katie smirked.

"Oh!" Katie exclaimed, startling Damian. "I know where I want to eat! The Hard Rock Café."

Damian looked at her. "Haven't you been to the one in Las Vegas?"

"Yeah, but I've heard it's not as cool as this one." Katie put her hands together in supplication. "*Pleeeeease?*"

"Yeah, yeah." Damian laughed, pulling up the map app on his phone to work out which way they needed to walk. "Hard Rock it is."

"Yay." Katie almost skipped along.

While Katie and Damian made their way to the restaurant, talking animatedly about the stars and the sights, a couple of cops were walking toward them, discussing past night shifts they had been on.

The two were on patrol, and it had been relatively quiet up to that point—which was strange for Hollywood. They went through things on-shift that happened nowhere else in the country, except maybe Vegas…or New York. There was a lot of crazy shit in Vegas twenty-four hours a day, and New York was just a clusterfuck of crazy crammed onto a small island.

"Yeah, so I arrested this chick. Total freak," the cop on the left explained. "She was in the back of the squad car screaming out lyrics to some old-ass AC/DC song, totally topless."

"This place gets weirder and weirder," the other cop replied, shaking his head. "What did you pick her up for?"

"That's the fucking kicker," he commented, and dipped his hat to a young boy who was pointing at the officer. "I picked her up for spray-painting a sign over on Fifth. She was completely clothed when she got in the car, then started doing *Girls Gone Wild*. I don't even know how she got her top open, to be honest."

"At least she wasn't the crazy fat lady from that

Halloween bust." His partner laughed. "Holy shit, that was the scariest thing I've ever seen."

"Hey, look! Isn't that…." The cop pointed toward Katie and Damian.

"Part of the D squad," his partner whispered. "No *fucking* way."

"This is Officer Chavez," the first officer murmured quietly into his radio.

"Go ahead," the operator replied.

"I just wanted to know if there was anything strange going down," he asked. "I just spotted part of the D squad roaming around here in Hollywood."

"That's a negative, Chavez," the operator told him. "They are just there to enjoy themselves. Out."

Chavez shrugged. "Well, I guess everyone needs a bit of a vacation from time to time."

As they passed Katie and Damian, a call came over their system. They unintentionally stopped just a few feet away to listen to the voice on the other end. It was a serious call, and not a welcome one.

"All available units to First Republic Bank. We have a 444 and a 211S in progress," the operator advised.

"Chavez and Simon, following up," Chavez informed Central.

"Copy that," the operator acknowledged. "Be advised that the suspects are armed, and very dangerous. Do not provoke."

"Copy," Chavez said, signing off and popping Simon on his shoulder. "It's time to get our jog on."

Katie glanced up as the cops ran past them. She was thinking about those call identifiers. Damian looked at her, knowing that the call of duty was pulsing through her veins.

She bit her lip and looked at the shop window.

"A 444 is an officer-involved shooting," she whispered to Damian. "And a 211S is a burglar alarm—the silent one. Someone is robbing a bank, and whoever it was took down a cop—which was a terrible move on their part."

Damian's head swiveled to track her as she started walking faster and faster in the direction the cops had gone.

She was nearly jogging when Damian sighed and ran to catch up.

She was so bad with things like that. She wanted to save the world, demon-related or not. She would have been one hell of a cop or soldier in her civilian life, that was for sure. Still, they were there to relax, not to chase down every perp on the street.

That was what the cops were for.

Damian's cross bounced against his chest beneath his shirt as he trotted after Katie, and he was out of breath.

"Got to," he huffed, "do more cardio!" He dodged between a couple of cars and Katie did something where she put a hand on the hood of a car and vaulted over, managing to accomplish a somersault with full twist in the air. "Oh, that's so much bullshit!" he grumped when she landed gracefully and kept running.

Training it was, or he was gonna get fat and sloppy fast. He picked up the pace while looking up to the heavens.

"Was it too much to ask for a *quiet* afternoon?"

Three more cop cars came to a sliding stop at the bank. There were at least a dozen already, and a gaggle of onlookers that was growing larger by the second. The police had the place surrounded, but they weren't positive what they should do next.

Chavez and Simon, who had gotten there on foot, bent over, hands on their knees, trying to catch their breath. Katie and Damian were only a few steps behind but were stopped by the ropes. Police crowd control was using the barrier to push the crowd back a little at a time.

"It's a bank robbery," Damian whispered between breaths. "Not really our line of work unless the robber has red eyes and snarls, Katie."

"How would we know unless we went in?" Katie asked, watching wide-eyed from the ropes before turning to Damian. "Besides, Korbin said they might need our help on a bunch of different issues."

He raised an eyebrow, "I don't think he meant listening to the speaker on a cop's vest and then ambulance-chasing them to the scene of the crime," Damian replied.

She patted him on the chest before turning back. "All in the details, my friend."

"Christ almighty!" a tall detective in a suit exclaimed, throwing his hands into the air and walking toward the cop pushing the people back. "*SMITH*, you got people creeping the barrier forward, for fuck's sake. You have got to show some balls here and get them to move back. These people should not be in the middle of this situation."

"Yes sir," the young cop said, walking forward.

The detective glanced at the crowd and looked away, but before he could take another step he froze.

Slowly he turned back and stared at Katie and Damian. He knew exactly who they were, but what in the world were they doing at *his* crime scene? Was there something he didn't know about what was in that building?

"You and you." The detective pointed at Katie and Damian and waved them toward him. "Come with me. The rest of you, push back so that if there's gunfire we don't accidently blow your brains all over the sidewalk...*please!*"

Katie chuckled at his attempt to be nice by using please at the end of a sentence like that. They ducked under the ropes and followed the detective to his unmarked car, which had a temp light flashing on top. There was a layout of the bank on the trunk, and a pile of cigarette butts on the ground.

"Look, I don't know what is going on in there," he said quietly, looking at the two of them before glancing around to make sure no one was sneaking a listen. "It probably doesn't have a damn thing to do with your D Squad stuff, but there are a lot of people in that bank—and some of them are children."

"What do you know so far?" Katie eyes flitted over to the bank.

"I was kind of wondering the same thing about the two of you," he admitted. "Why are you here...at this specific crime scene?"

"No reason," Damian answered. "We heard it over the speaker of some cops standing next to us, and we figured maybe you guys could use an extra couple of hands. We know what an ambush looks like, but we also know that in this climate they may kill someone innocent if it takes us too long. We really aren't sure what to do, though. What is your take on the situation inside?"

"One officer, who had a second job at the bank, was shot. No idea how severe the injury is, but shot is shot," the detective answered. "There are a lot of innocent people in there, so we are afraid to barge in and risk lives. For whatever reason, we have two other issues going on the West side, so our negotiators are stuck in those locations right now. I know you guys are trained in tactical and you've faced some serious shit, so will you help us?"

Katie and Damian looked at each other and shrugged, and Damian nodded. Katie smiled and patted him on the shoulder, happy he was going to back her up.

She turned back to the detective and stuck out her hand. The cop let out a deep breath and shook it, obviously relieved that he wouldn't have to rely on his underpaid and overworked cops to get all the hostages out of that dangerous situation. He didn't want to be the one who cost innocent people their lives.

"We'll help, but it has to be on our terms," Katie advised him. "We need a bit of freedom to take care of this."

"You got whatever you need; all the freedom in the world," he assured her. "We don't need senseless deaths on our hands, and we need to get that injured cop out of there, so we can get him to help.

"Detective," the captain began, walking over. "Where are we on this? And who are these two?"

The detective waited for the man to get closer. "Captain, this is Damian and Katie—part of the D Squad," he replied. "They've agreed to help us out on this."

"Oh, shit," the captain said with wide eyes. "I like the

sound of that! Anything you need… We got tactical teams, blueprints of the building… You need it, just ask and we'll get it for you."

"All right," Katie said, rubbing her hands together. "Let's come up with a plan."

The four of them gathered around the back of the car, and Katie started laying out the plan for them. She didn't see any difference between these guys and a demon, and for all she knew a demon was behind this.

The day had started as a vacation, but the adrenaline pumping through her told her this shit was in her blood. With Pandora and Damian on her side, she was fairly sure these assholes didn't have a chance in…

Well, *hell.*

5

"The layout is simple," Stephanie told Korbin as she unfolded her blueprints on Korbin's desk. "There is one large building in the center that has an aboveground floor and an underground location pretty deep below. There is a ventilation system that pumps in good air, and it runs through the entire bottom level. Along the right side of the main ICBM building are barracks, mostly low-grade rooms for the plebes who worked the base. To the left is a larger barracks; maybe ten or twelve rooms, all upstairs. They look like they were officers' quarters."

"Are they livable now?" Korbin asked.

"Yeah, they are in decent shape, actually," Stephanie replied. "The barracks also has a basement with a compression chamber that leads to the next main ventilated areas, so if there was an emergency they could go to the underground chambers."

"What about medical?" Korbin asked.

"Across the back here is a long rectangular building that seems to have been the hospital," Stephanie said, pointing to the map. "Things are still intact, but it was stripped. It needs straightening up and a real good clean, and then you have yourself a hospital. Now, I don't know about holding facilities for things like demons, but there *are* radiation rooms."

"That's not a big deal." Korbin rubbed his jaw, taking a few moments to study the plans. "We can build those. They are specialty places for us, anyway. I just want to make sure there is room for all of us when we move. We can't wait until the new base is finished, but we can stay aboveground until we are sure the ventilation system is still in tip-top shape."

"Right." Stephanie stood up. "We can test all that stuff in a few hours' time. I've done some exploring, but I haven't really pushed the envelope too much. I bought the land thinking I'd perhaps turn it into a larger brothel— almost a camp for adults—but never got around to the restoration."

"Good for us." Korbin smiled.

"Yeah." She scoffed. "I didn't like the business anyways, and I'm pretty sure that's why I never actually got around to it. I didn't want a bunny ranch, I wanted a life."

"Well, now you have one, though it's not as free as you might be otherwise." Korbin smiled. "I just need us back up and running, but we can't go there if we can't get it into service relatively quickly."

"Everything aboveground just needs to be cleaned." Stephanie tapped a finger on the desk, thinking. "Maybe some light bulbs replaced, bedroom stuff, moving racks out, but all in all it just needs a loving touch—nothing the boys and girls can't handle. There is also an underground bunker back here that is camouflaged to avoid detection from the sky and at ground-level. I was thinking it might be a good place for the business."

"That sounds interesting," Korbin mused. "We will definitely take a look at that as soon as we get over there."

"I think that with everyone's help, we could have this whole facility—or whatever is left of it—moved in a couple days' time." Stephanie looked up at him. "Three, tops."

"We could spend one day moving this main building floor by floor, and then one day getting anything salvageable out of the extra buildings." Korbin considered the layout of the buildings. "Yeah, I don't think it will take too long, and everyone is ready to get out of this mess. I think living in a dust bowl is starting to get to them. When they train they get covered in dust, and when they go to bed they have to wipe everything off again. It's kind of a pain in the ass, that's for damn sure."

Stephanie laughed. "I know, remember? I live here now."

"Yeah." Korbin chuckled. "I forget sometimes."

As if, he chided himself.

"Anyway, I think I could get the girls to come help. Do some painting, get things looking nice the way we did here," Stephanie continued. "I can get construction crews to start ventilating the shafts underneath, and clearing out any debris we can't use. That will give us a clean slate to work with. There is nothing worse than getting it all cleaned up and having piles of shit lying around. Get it all hauled off before anything secret comes in there and we can't let the crews on the base."

"That's smart," he admitted. "I want our new place to be treated like a top-secret military installation, because... well, that's really what it is. It's a place to keep everything under control; under lock and key. I want to figure out some way to camouflage it from the sky even better, if it needs it. I don't want people coming in and out without proper clearance. We have to get serious about this. We saw what happened when we treated this place like a normal house. We were attacked in our own damned yard. It could have been disastrous, and in some ways, it was. In other ways, it made me realize what I need to be doing; what this place is missing. It has become too relaxed."

"I agree with you on that," she told him. "I loved the feeling of family, but we didn't treat it like there was any danger."

"Absolutely," Korbin replied. "When we lost that edge, that deep-seated fear that we all have, we got careless. Carelessness caused Jeremy to get killed. I think this team has seen enough death in the time they've been here to last them the rest of their lives. I'd like a good long streak where I don't have to worry about funerals, memorials, and grief. I just want to move forward into a new and stronger day with a fresh start, and I think this move is what might do it. If we all work together, we can get what we need out of the base and start building what we want. There definitely hasn't been a lack of business or payments recently."

"Very true," Stephanie agreed, folding up the blueprints. "Well, I can get some construction companies over to the site and meet with them as soon as *now*."

Korbin put up a hand. "Hold off just a little bit longer."

He nodded toward their kitchen. "The team leaders are still here, and I don't want to leave them on their own. There is too much going on, and too many slip-ups could occur. When they are gone—and I mean the moment they board their plane—I will be out of here too. We all will. We will jump right into getting the place set up and ready to move into. It's been a hard road—and there is still a lot to contend with—but at least we know that we will soon have a strong, reliable home to come back to. We will be able to work more efficiently, and we will be able to do better at tracking and running the current calls we get. It just takes time."

"That it does." Stephanie smiled. "Anyway, you have some people to entertain, and a nap is calling my name. Come and get me when they are gone. I want to show you around the base, and get some contractors out for you to talk to."

"I will." Korbin grinned at her. "And one day I'll actually try that resting thing, too."

Ella Hamilton was *that* girl—that New York City twenty-year-old still living with her parents.

Her long hair was wildly streaked pink and purple, her makeup was dark and crazy no matter what time of day it was, and her attitude matched all of the above. She was a wild child, and had been her whole life.

Her parents weren't home ninety percent of the time, and the other ten they drove her absolutely fucking batshit crazy.

She was teetering on the edge of no future, walking the edge of a homeless, jobless, or perhaps addicted life—and she didn't give two shits about it.

The craziest part of it all was that Ella was extremely smart; possibly genius-level, she had been told. But all she wanted to do was drink, smoke, and party as much as she possibly could.

"Yeah, right. Whatever, Mom," she yelled over her shoulder, tramping down the sidewalk in her combat boots, torn jeans, and military jacket. "Fucking *parents!*" she huffed, disgusted.

She threw her Starbucks shirt and hat in her bag as she walked to the cab. She was annoyed by her mother; someone she felt she barely knew, someone who drove her fucking nuts on a regular basis. She wasn't a momma's girl, and she barely ever spoke to her father. She just wanted them to leave her the hell alone.

"My life can't *possibly* get any fucking worse," she grumbled as she climbed into the cab.

She was never early to work. In fact she was usually lucky to even show up, but she somehow managed to not get fired.

Her awakening with her mother, though, had been so insane that she was actually leaving early for work that day.

She had been happily asleep—passed out, to be exact—from the party she had been to the night before, but at the butt-crack of dawn her mother went on one of her rampages, waking her up and bitching about every little thing.

She had told her parental unit the same thing she

always did; that she couldn't be a mother only when she wanted to, that she had given that right up a long time before, but of course that didn't fly. It never did.

Her mother had been tipped over the edge by it, and it just went on and on until Ella grabbed her shit and headed out the door.

Ella gave the cabbie her work address and sat in the back looking out the window.

She had always known she would go down that path; she had made it a point to do so. She was fucking smart and she knew she had control, but when her parents started going nuts and life just got to be too much, she had buried herself in the underground. She lost her pain in drugs and alcohol, danced until her feet couldn't move anymore, and fell into the arms of whatever hottie was crushing on her that night.

Self-respect wasn't the name of her game, nor was respect.

She was upfront about it, and she wasn't worried what others thought. She didn't give a flying fuck, and that was just how it was. There was no fucking way she was going to bend to the demands of her society or her parents, who didn't do anything but bitch and push her further down the partying rabbit hole.

When the taxi pulled up in front of the coffee shop, she paid the driver in crumpled bills and got out, walking nonchalantly in the door.

The place was always packed, but so was everything else in New York. That was why she loved it there; there were always so many people. She could get lost in the crowds, and no one ever cared who the hell she was or what her story was. She put on her apron and tied her hair back before walking behind the counter and clocking in at the register.

"Wow!" Her supervisor looked at the non-existent watch on her wrist and back at Ella. "One minute early. I never thought I would see the day you got to work on time."

Ella gave her a fake smile and waited for her boss to turn back around. When she did she gave her the bird, mocking her expression with her own.

She hated that bitch. She was always so perfect, so innocent; so on-point with everything in life. She hadn't liked Ella even before she knew she was a slacker. She didn't dress the right way for her, her hair was never perfect enough, her makeup was never trendy enough, and Ella's personality sure as hell wasn't saccharine enough for that girl.

Her supervisor had tried to get her fired several times, but the manager wouldn't let it happen. He was a friend of her mother's somehow, and had promised to keep her on no matter what.

So she was always scheduled as an extra, just in case she didn't show up for a shift.

Ella took a deep breath and asked the person standing at the register what she could get for them.

She put the order into the computer and sent it back, taking the payment and offering a very fake and obviously sarcastic thank you to the woman. When the next girl stepped up Ella paused, noticing strange red rings in her eyes. At first they almost mesmerized her, but then she was slightly freaked out.

"Welcome to Starbucks," she said in a monotone. "May I take your order?"

"I'll have a Venti Chai over ice, five pumps, soy milk, with a dollop of whipped cream on top." The girl sounded almost like a robot herself. "Not too much whipped cream; just enough to sweeten the drink a little bit," she finished.

Ella watched the girl talk, wondering what the hell was wrong with her.

She shook the thought from her head and put the drink order in the computer, thankful she didn't have to make that one. She hated it when complicated orders came in, though she almost felt like this girl might rip your throat out—literally—if the dollop of whipped cream was too big or too small.

"I'd also like a piece of crumb cake," she added.

"*Okaaay,* that is a Venti Chai latte, iced, five pumps, soy milk, and a not too big yet not too small dollop of whipped cream," Ella repeated slowly. "And crumb cake."

The girl nodded.

"That will be eleven-nineteen," Ella replied.

Ella pulled the crumb cake from the shelf, sliding it into one of the wax-coated brown baggies they served all their baked goods in. She waited for the girl to complete the signature on the keypad, then handed her the cake.

"Oh, what name do you want on this?" Ella asked.

"Bridgett," she answered as she walked away.

"Okay." Ella pursed her lips. "R-for-robot dot Bridgett it is."

She handed the cup to another barista and turned back to the register, more irritated than she had been before for some reason.

She was usually the one people thought was weird, but Ella knew there were some serious freaks in her city. She didn't know what Bridgett's story was, but she wouldn't want to run into her in a dark club—that was for damn sure.

She could feel the irritation rising as she took the next order, the stereotypical white midlife-crisis mom standing at the counter wearing tennis clothes when she knew damn well she didn't play tennis.

She turned quickly to pass the cup, and caught a whiff of herself.

Damn, I'm going to have to shower. What a pain in the ass!

6

Damian whistled. One hand was in his pocket, and his other arm was around Katie's waist. She had done her hair and makeup, and they pranced down the block. It was all part of the plan; she had to get the robbers to think that she had no clue what was going on. As they passed in front of the cops, the loud speaker crackled and the captain's voice came over the intercom.

"Please halt!" he called right before they hit the doors. "Do not go into the bank! We repeat, do *not* go into the bank. There is an active shooter inside." There was a pause before he turned, bullhorn still active, "Can they hear me, or are they just idiots?" he asked, and a few onlookers snickered in the crowd.

Damian and Katie acted like they didn't hear the police officer and walked straight into the large brick building, talking and smiling at one another.

Katie noticed the people on the ground, but acted oblivious, as did Damian.

She made a comment about her clothes and laughed loudly, ignoring the fact that her voice carried through the strange silence of the bank, and Damian chattered back. Katie actually found the whole thing to be amusing.

"Hey," one of the robbers called, but Katie and Damian ignored him. "*HEY!* Shut the fuck up, you two!"

"Huh? Oh!" Katie stopped and looking around in surprise. "Oh my goodness, are we in a *MOVIE?*" she squealed.

She clapped her hands and giggled excitedly.

"No, you stupid Valley Girl," the guy snarled, starting toward her and waving his pistol. "This is fucking real life, you dumb-assed bitch. Now *get on the floor.*"

Wait, what the fuck is a Valley Girl? Pandora asked.

It's a really rich, really dumb girl who grows up in privilege and has no idea about life, Katie replied, looking at the hooded men with big eyes.

Oh, HELLLL no, Pandora growled. *He did* not *just call me a dumb-ass blonde. This dude is going to fucking get it.*

Wait for it, Katie told her. *You will have your moment.*

Damian looked around like he was completely confused, swatting at one of the guys when he pushed Damian down onto one knee.

He looked up at the main guy, who was walking quickly toward Katie. She had a look of innocence on her face that forced him to smirk. He tilted his head down to avoid being seen smiling. Katie watched the man as he approached, tilting her head to the side like a Valley Girl would.

"Oh my Gawd, is that a gun?" she asked. She noted that Damian was trying not to laugh.

"That's right, dumb-ass," the robber growled, raising the butt to hit her in the head.

"Oh no, Mr. Robber, please don't," she called as he cocked his hand back.

He was shocked when her arm darted up to catch the gun as he swung downward.

She has a snarl on her lips and the ring in her eyes flashed red as she lifted her head and looked the guy right in the eyes. His grimace smoothed and he looked at her strangely when he felt the strength in her arm as she pushed his hand back.

"Now, that wasn't very *nice*," she hissed, shaking her head. The last word came out in a deep growl.

Katie grabbed the guy by his throat and lifted him into the air.

His feet were dangling, and he kicked as his hands grabbed hers, trying to unlock her grip.

Her eyes were completely red as she stared up at him.

"You," he wheezed, "are a crazy bitch!" His eyes bugged out in terror as Pandora laughed wildly inside Katie. She threw him hard, and he slammed into the wall and fell in a heap to the floor.

She turned and found Damian fighting one of the other robbers, punching him right in the face. She smiled and looked at a third perp, who had raised his gun to shoot Damian and was waiting for an opening. She threw one of the knives from her belt, and the blade turned end over end before sinking deep into his bicep. He screamed in pain, dropping the gun to the floor and grabbing his arm as he knelt.

She looked back just as Damian kicked the robber's feet out from under him, sending him spiraling to the floor. He grabbed a metal divider post from beside the wooden island in the middle of the bank floor and swung it over his head, hitting the guy hard and obliterating his consciousness.

Breathing heavily, he dropped the pole and walked over to the one who was writhing over the knife in his arm. Katie walked over too and looked at Damian.

"Hold on just one second," she said, reaching down and yanking the knife out.

"*FUUCK!*" the robber screamed and brought his arm to his chest, almost crying. "You stupid fucking bitch!"

"It's not very nice to talk about a man's wife in that manner," Damian told him in a conversational tone before turning to Katie. "Honey, would you like to do the honors?"

"Oh, please, be my guest." She smirked.

Damian cold-cocked the guy, watching as his eyes rolled back in his head and he crumpled to the ground. Quickly they pulled the three perps into a pile in the middle of the floor. Katie raised her dress to reveal her tactical belt, pants, and walkie-talkie as Damian used a belt to slow the perp's bleeding.

"Be advised, all three suspects are down," Katie said into the walkie-talkie. "We will be sending the hostages out."

Katie pointed to Damian, to the hostages, and to the door, then ran over and got people to their feet.

Quickly she ushered them toward the entrance, looking

out into the street before opening the doors and sending them out one by one. The police ran forward, accepting the hostages and pulling them to safety.

"We are making sure they are safe," the captain said. "Good work in there, you two."

Katie smiled at Damian and tossed him the walkie-talkie, then ran to the back to see if she could find the downed cop. She found him back near the vault, leaning against a wall with a t-shirt wrapped tightly around his arm. He had lost a lot of blood, but the wound didn't look life-threatening.

"Who are you?" he moaned.

She leaned closer, so she could speak without the civilians overhearing. "Part of the D Squad."

"Holy shit," he whispered back, staring at her. "Why? This wasn't demon-related."

"Just in the right place at the right time, I suppose." She smiled.

There were two people taking care of him. She nodded, and they leaned down and helped him to his feet. Slowly they walked him forward, stopping in front of Katie when he did.

"Thank you," he told her earnestly. "You saved a lot of people's lives."

Katie just smiled. She waited until he had disappeared through the door to nod. She felt good about helping those people; about getting them to safety.

He was hot, Pandora offered. *Even with a hole in his arm.*

Not now. Katie turned back.

Katie walked back to Damian, who nodded toward the back door. There was no reason to go back out there and talk to the cops. They had finished their job. Katie went out first, almost skipping again, and Damian laughed as he followed her.

I think I deserve some donuts, Pandora announced.

I thought you gave donuts up? Katie asked.

I did, for two whole horribly insane days, she griped in exasperation. *I deserve an extra box for self-control beyond normal expectations.*

All right. Katie chuckled. *I've got just the place.*

Katie took Damian and her pain-in-the-ass roomie to Kettle Glazed Donuts, one of the most varietal donut shops in the city.

She had looked up donut shops before coming to LA, since being prepared was half the battle with Pandora.

As soon as they walked into the glass-fronted shop with the little red stools at the window-side counter, Pandora lost her fucking mind. In the display cases were towers of handmade perfection, dripping with every topping you could imagine.

She was in donut heaven.

You can't fight it! Pandora sniffed wildly, using Katie's nose. *You* shouldn't *fight it.* Please *don't fight it, and I'll be your friend forever.*

I am getting you one dozen, and that's it, Katie told her firmly.

You already got your mad out, and I had nothing to do with you beating the shit out of that robber, Pandora grumbled as she looked at the choices, trying to figure out how to limit the list to just twelve.

You are a bitch! A stone-cold bitch.

"Hey, Bridgett." Melvin nodded. He noticed her sunglasses as he walked up to the table. "How's it going?"

"Hey." She forced a smile. "It's going good. Please sit down. Thanks for meeting me here on such short notice."

"It's no problem. What's up?" He slid into a chair at her table.

Melvin Ransom was the team heavy for the Wyld Jokers, a group of ruthless killers hell-bent on ridding New York City of demons.

Melvin had a special-ops background and a lust for killing those who shouldn't exist. He was a pusher; a guy who wanted to be top of the pack, but knew exactly what he was best at.

He killed them, but politics—they just weren't his thing. He didn't know why this chick he had barely said two words to would want to talk to him, but he'd figured, why not? What was the worst that could come of it?

"I'll cut right to the chase." She lowered her voice and looked around. "We both know you are in the demon business. That's no secret to me."

"It's not?" He chuckled.

"I know someone who wants to help move things along for you," she continued. "In exchange for providing me with information, I can give you information on attacks; ones you may otherwise have no idea are coming."

He sat back in his chair, looking as if he was thinking things over. Bridgett removed her glasses, dropping them in her bag, and fixed her hair. She quickly looked up and to the side, letting Melvin see her red-ringed eyes. He breathed deeply, now understanding what was going on.

"All right." He looked around before returning his gaze to her and nodding. "But we can't talk about this here. Meet me in the alley in ten minutes."

He glanced toward the door. "You leave that way. I'll meet you around back."

She smiled and stood up, walking nonchalantly out the door with her coffee in hand. He sat there for a few minutes mulling over her offer, sipping his coffee and watching the other patrons.

After sitting there for a little while, he got up and walked past the bathrooms and straight out the back door, making a mental note where the security camera was. Bridgett smiled as he approached, excited for once to be part of the action. She had waited a long time for this chance. He walked very close to her and leaned in.

"You see, Bridgett, there are only three options," he whispered, like a lover might. "Dead, research, or on a *team*." He grabbed her quickly by the neck. "At least for those who have *tamed* demons inside."

Bridgett's eyes went wide and she grabbed his hand, clawing like crazy to get free. The demon inside her roared in anger and forced her to fight back.

She brought her legs up, jamming them hard into his groin to make him let her go. She landed in a crouch, growling, her eyes now completely red and her expression wild. She ran forward to swipe at his chest; her hands now had small claws. He jumped back, chuckling as she attacked, and whistled at the power in her.

"Wow," he taunted. "You must have a *hell* of demon

inside you, sweetheart. Let's see if we can't get you some help."

"I don't want your help," she hissed. "I want your head!"

She ran forward with her claws out, slashing through the air. He put his hands up and she grabbed his gun from his holster. His eyes went turned as she backed up, pointing the weapon at his chest. She clicked off the safety and smiled maniacally, ready to do her demon's bidding.

"You know," Melvin began, shaking his finger and moving carefully to his right, "I *thought* there was something weird about you calling me. You see, I don't have any close friends in this city since my line of work makes it a little bit difficult, but I thought to myself, Melvin, how many times does a pretty girl you've run into a couple of times at the library call you out of the blue and ask you out for coffee? The answer, if you're wondering, is not that often, so I came. I have to say, you definitely surprised me. I did *not* peg you for a drooling nasty soul-sucking-demon-ridden hag, that's for sure. But then again, you wouldn't be the first one I dated. Women in general tend to carry the gene, I think."

"Shut up," she growled, circling around him.

Just then, a girl wearing a Starbuck's apron and ripped black jeans, with wildly colored hair and heavy makeup, came out the back door carrying the trash.

She didn't immediately see them, since she was watching where she was going. She was bitching up a storm, and it distracted Bridgett enough to make her turn toward the girl.

Melvin leapt into action. He jumped behind her and

grabbed her chin and the back of her head and twisted, quickly snapping her neck.

He had wanted to help her, but he could see that her demon had latched on hard and she was liable to shoot the girl who had come out of the building.

The girl gasped and froze, unsure what she had just witnessed.

Ivy, the demon inside Bridgett, panicked, finding himself being dragged down with the soul of the girl who had just died.

"FUCKING HELL!" He hated rash actions, but he quickly jumped out of her body, not at all prepared to be in the real world. He raced over to the only uninfected body he could find and dove down Ella's throat.

Melvin watched wide-eyed as Starbucks Girl stiffened and dropped the bags of trash, her eyes flashing red before they rolled back in her head.

He lunged forward, catching her as she fainted and fell from the stairs. He sadly held her in his arms, knowing she had just been infected.

Dammit! It was not his day in any way, shape, or form.

"Fucking hell," he growled, pulling his phone from his pocket.

He called his supervisor Isaac, since the team lead was visiting one of the other compounds. He was pissed—beyond pissed—that the demons had lowered themselves to that level. Two girls, young and attractive—their lives ripped away because of one asshole demon.

Isaac chuckled as he answered. "Melvin, how is that coffee date going?"

"Uh, well, she's dead," he answered. "So I'd have to say

it's been pretty shitty. Listen, I need backup to come for the bodies. She was a demon and she wanted me to spy on the teams, so naturally I told her to go to hell…and then I sent her there."

"You said 'bodies,' plural," Isaac asked, calling out commands in the background.

"Yeah, the demon jumped into another girl before it could be pulled back to hell," he told Isaac. "She's passed-out in my arms, and let me tell you right now…" he stared down at her wild makeup and crazily-colored hair, "she looks like a wild one."

Isaac sighed. "Well then, she'll fit in just fine with us."

7

"He is dead, sir," the servant said.

"Dead?" T'Chezz said whipping around. "What do you mean? He was the best we had. Well, the *only* one we fucking had, and you are telling me he couldn't survive a month on Earth? For fuck's sake! Are we *sure* he's dead?"

"Yes, master," he said, bowing his head in fear. "I went up to check on him after Zallot returned, as you asked me to do, and I saw the demon's dead human body being loaded into an SUV. It was one of the killers, but not your sister's team this time; another one in a different city. I left my host's body and came straight back to report to you."

"And you saw no one else?" he asked. "He couldn't have maybe jumped hosts to one of the Damned?"

"The only ones I saw were infested with low-level demons," the servant replied. "No one else."

"Pity. "T'Chezz sighed, twirling his black brittle goatee around his finger. "That means he didn't accept our offer.

The Killers, even the weakest ones, have more self-control than most humans, which I find both disgusting and interesting at the same time."

"Occasionally they are cunning, Your Grace," the servant sniveled.

"Yes.' T'Chezz reached up to pull a piece of lunch out of his teeth. "Remind me to torture that Damned for a significant amount of time when I get Earth-side. Oh well, no use in crying over spilled humans. Let's pick another. I can't believe they are all as moral and incorruptible as that ass. Someone on those fucking teams can be turned; they *are* humans, after all. If they can be convinced to buy expensive jewelry and little boxes for their human bodies when they die, they can be convinced of this. I offer more than just jewels. I *will* find my human, even if I have to go there myself."

T'Chezz turned back to the servant and found him eyeing the ball of metal.

He had kept it there as a daily reminder of the hatred he had for the human race—and for his sister, whom he hadn't forgotten about for a moment. He needed to find the weapons, and he knew that when he found them he would find *her*. There was little doubt in his mind that she was connected to all of it; her and that pathetic useless body she had attached herself to.

"I kept it," T'Chezz answered the unasked question. "I was told that it was a Ferrari California T model, a very expensive car on Earth—at least it was before it hit me. I crushed it in my frustration, as you know." His smile was all teeth. "I'm saving it for my sister, so I can shove it up her ass without lube. I do hope some of the jagged edges rust before I do that."

He smiled and turned toward the window, a happy feeling taking him over as he thought about the horrible things he would do to his sister when he found her.

He still hadn't decided if he would do it to her human too, or wait until he got her back down in the depths of hell. Either way, it was going to be a very good day when he finally had that bitch back in his claws.

"Will they kill demons?" Amy asked, looking at the blade of a sword.

"They kill just like any other weapon of that quality," Korbin replied. "The difference is, one slash from one of these and the demon is temporarily stunned and screaming in pain, which provides you the opportunity to deploy more tactics. Now, we also use a cross made from this metal, and it melts the head right off the demons, but they have to be weakened first. We are also working on turning this material into bullets."

"That would be *fantastic*," John exclaimed, holding up a sword.

Initially the idea was to *give* the first weapons to the other teams, but as he watched them, he realized there was no reason to pass up a profit.

Korbin grabbed a piece of paper from his pocket and reviewed it quickly; it was the markup on the weapons he had been working on with Joshua, Stephanie, and Katie. It was the price-point at which he was willing to sell to the other mercenaries, but it still gave them a profit.

"I obviously have to have these," Amy told him. "But what are the prices?"

"The weapons are priced between $35k and $55k if we keep government out of it." Korbin shrugged. "If they get involved, the prices will go up and the quantity will go down."

Amy nodded. "Sounds fair."

"Indeed," William agreed, shaking his head. "I've paid more for normal swords that snap when pushed into a tough demon body. There aren't many weapons out there that give us an edge on these beasts—and until recently that was okay. We had our soldiers, but now things are changing. Normal tactics aren't enough to get us through these encounters anymore. The demons are getting bigger, and the infected humans we can save have gotten thin on the ground, since most of these demons are taking hold of them too deeply to get them back."

"I'm not bullshitting you on this," Korbin warned, stepping forward. "If the government so much as sniffs around, all these goodies are going to stop being available. Higher-ups control most things, but in the end we are mercenaries, not slaves."

"It hasn't been so bad lately," Brian commented. "In fact, we have been working with the police and the DEA on a lot of things."

"Us too," Amy added. "And wasn't it the CIA or the FBI or one of those organizations that helped get your men to Los Angeles during that last incursion that flattened that cemetery?"

"They did," Korbin agreed, "but do not forget that they have to take orders. They would turn around and shoot us in the back of the head if they were told to. We take for granted that we are family; that we help each other first, and voluntarily do the right thing. The government is not like that, and I don't want you to fall for their kind words and amazing gestures. They need us right now, but when they don't they will turn on us. They have before, and they will again."

Korbin picked up a sword and examined the blade closely.

"I don't want to become a vassal to the state," Korbin continued. "I know how much the international budget for fighting demons is, and we know the US government has their own teams doing it too. There is no other way to produce these, and I'm not going to share. I don't trust the government to have my best interests or the best interests of my team at heart—or yours, for that matter. We are the ones out here doing the back-breaking work, losing people and finding answers. When is the last time you saw or even heard of one of the government teams taking out a horde of normal demons, much less one or two of the larger bastards? Where were they when we needed them in Los Angeles? They were *nowhere*, and sure as shit they weren't jumping on any backs cutting demons' necks."

"He's right." William looked at the other leads. "I haven't heard that any of their teams has ever made a big catch. It's been all small stuff, and when it matters and shit goes down, they never seem to show."

"Yeah." John sighed. "You may be right. We might be mercenaries, but we have the lock on the demon-slaying thing. If the government finds out about this stuff they may try to seize the weapons, and getting some back will be like pulling teeth. They will equip their men first, and then throw the bones to us—even though we are the ones who have kept shit in the W column for decades."

"You won't hear a peep out of me," Amy agreed. "This is too important. I've seen the destruction, I've been to the ceremonies, and I know what your team and all the others do to keep ourselves afloat without the government's help with anything besides money."

"That's why they pay so well for demons." Brian chuckled. "They aren't giving us any money to operate without quid pro quo, so they know we will have to spend our own."

"I've heard there is a new general in place over the government teams," William shared. "They say that he has a better attitude about working with mercenary teams; that he recognizes the importance of what we do, and were doing long before the government was as focused as they are now. I don't know if that means anything, but I am hoping we can get some assistance when we need it. Give the tools to those of us who actually do the job."

"Sounds better than the last guy, who actually tried to shut us down." Amy shook her head. "I was convinced the bastard was a demon himself."

"Yeah." Korbin nodded. "I'll believe that the general is on our side when it happens—and continues to happen through more than one incursion. Maybe five ops in a row will change my mind. I've been around a long time, and I have to say that it's complete bullshit; how they keep bringing us in and pushing us back out. We are the ugly stepsisters of the demon war, and it's time that changed."

"Preach it!" Amy waved the knife she was holding in the air and the metal shimmered in the light.

"I have to be honest, though: it would be a lot easier if we did have a good relationship with the military side," Korbin continued. "I mean, at least then we would be *given* the tools to protect each other, instead of selling them to those who are going to be on the front lines. It feels almost demeaning, in a way. 'We know you are going to save our asses, but you have to buy the weapons from me to do it.' It's total bullshit!"

"Ah, the American economic system." William laughed. "It's so fucked up that it is backward; no one can fully understand it. Nothing changes, which makes it difficult for me to continue to watch it happen. I mean, did no one notice that Armageddon is here? Demons on Earth? Sorry, that shit just gets me going."

"So far, all the government and military folks have wanted to do in the past was throw their weight around." Korbin sighed. "And I don't have time for ritual dick-measurement events."

Amy chuckled. "Nor do I."

Brian pointed to her. "You have the biggest one of all!"

"Very true," Amy agreed, putting her choices on the table. "All right, I will take these. Ring me up, sir."

"Two long swords and a dagger," Korbin tallied, writing up a receipt. "That will be $145k."

Amy pulled over a briefcase she had grabbed from the SUV and opened it, revealing the large amount of cash inside.

They couldn't write checks because that would alert the government, so they bought everything with cash. She always carried a couple hundred thousand with her. Just never knew when you would need it. It was kind of ridiculous, like a bad mobster movie, but it worked.

The rest of the team leaders made their selection, until all the weapons had not only been chosen but paid for as well.

In the end, Korbin racked up over half a million dollars from this one sales effort.

He put the money into a large bag and put it back into the safe, where he knew it would be secure. He closed the vault door and locked it, then turned back to the others. They looked excited; all were holding firmly to their weapons, staring at them with awe and excitement.

"Now I just have to figure out who to let use these. "Amy chuckled.

William shook his head. "Shit, these bitches are mine."

"I second that," Brian argued. "They will get the second set."

There was a knock, and Calvin stuck his face in. "Korbin," he called from the doorway, "the SUV is here to pick up the team leads and head back to the airport."

"Right," Korbin replied. "Perfect timing, actually."

"Good thing we rode the private jet," Amy joked. "I don't think they would let me carry these on the plane."

"Probably not." Korbin laughed. "Thank you, all, for coming. You all know how to reach me if you need more weapons. As soon as the bullets come out I will let you know, and if the groups' priests are interested in the killer cross, have them contact me."

The team leads shook Korbin's hand one at a time and headed out of the conference room single file, holding their new purchases high and proud. Korbin sat down and wiped his face as the leaders got into the SUV and headed for the airport.

He knocked on the door next to the conference room, and Stephanie and Joshua came out.

"How did it go?" Joshua asked.

"We sold every piece," Korbin confirmed.

"We decided to sell the pieces, not give them away?" he asked.

"I figured, why not? We made over half a million dollars," Korbin answered. "We can't fund this for everyone."

"Wow," Joshua exclaimed, his eyes big. "Well, I-I w-w-wanted to stop by and see how it went, but I know you two have business. I'm gonna get started on the next batch."

"Thanks, Joshua." Korbin waited as Stephanie hugged the younger man.

After Joshua had left the room and headed back down to his working space, Stephanie sat down in the chair in front of Korbin. She stretched her arms over her head and smiled, forcing a smile from him as well, then yawned and put her hands in her lap.

"The two of us have an appointment," she reminded him. "We are meeting a worker out at the land to lay some concrete."

"That was fast," Korbin admitted. "A lot faster than I had hoped."

"I told you...I *don't* mess around." She smiled. "You said you wanted to get out of here as soon as possible, so the girls are going there tomorrow to start cleaning the buildings at the new site."

"What would I do without you?"

"Sleep in a pile of rubble and go belly-up on your business?" she answered. "Anyway, we need to head out there now. He's probably already waiting for us."

"All right." Korbin groaned as he stood from his chair. "I only have one thing to say about the concrete: make it twice as big as you think it needs to be."

She nodded. "That can be arranged."

The two of them walked out of the conference room, looking around at the dust and debris that had fallen during the fight.

They were lucky they still had that side of the building to do business in, given how the empty buildings looked. Korbin was just glad Katie had decided to push the demon in that direction and not the other. It had probably been luck, but he had to start putting his confidence in her.

"This place looks terrible." Stephanie laughed and headed to the SUV.

Korbin opened the car door for her. "We are going to fix that problem really quickly."

8

After reluctantly deciding not to stay at the hotel in LA because the team leads had already left and hours of driving, Damian and Katie got back to the base.

Their place looked even spookier in the dark, like some lost and ruined civilization out in the sands.

There hadn't been any more sparking from the downed lights since the electricity had been cut to most of the buildings to avoid fires, but the moon's glow across the tumbled stones sent a shiver up Katie's spine.

She thought about that night. About losing a teammate, and about how everything had changed for her. She had found out new things about her powers, Korbin had started trusting her, and the team now looked to her for answers. She had never figured herself a leader, but that was what she was slowly turning into.

Damian parked the car and the two of them got out, then he went around back and opened the back doors.

"You going to do anything tonight?" Damian asked, grabbing his bags.

"Nope," Katie replied. "I am exhausted. I'm grabbing a shower, then heading to bed. You?"

"I have to update Korbin on the happenings of the day," he told her. "But first I will grab a shower too. I can still smell that disgusting robber's body odor on my hands. I swear, nobody takes showers anymore."

"They do." Katie laughed. "But unfortunately we only deal with the foulest of the bunch, so we may be out of luck finding a clean one."

"That's true, and yet sad at the same time. I mean, if I was a bad guy, I would still take a damn shower," Damian argued.

"I can see it now." Katie laughed. "Your description on the news is: tall, dark glasses, smells like Irish Spring."

"Damned right, but I guess I will see you in the morning." Damian waved and walked toward the door, but stopped. "I think I might get Korbin over with first. He is going to want to hear every gory detail of today's event, and update me on how things went with the leaders. I'm sure we will talk about it at the meeting, but you know how he is."

"Probably a good idea to talk to him now, and yes, I know exactly how he is." Katie smiled. "You are like the piece of paper he keeps notes on."

"Very true." He laughed and headed inside to make his way to Korbin's office after dropping his bag by the stairs.

Katie grabbed the door handle, but paused when she heard a voice behind her.

Stephanie, who was also coming back in for the night, was jogging across the lot to meet her.

She looked tired, but excited. Katie was glad to see her adjusting so well to her new life. Katie had worried about her at first, with so many changes going on: getting out of her business, taking over managing theirs, and becoming one of the Damned.

She looked completely different with her torn jeans and pink Chuck Taylors, but Katie liked it. Those clothes suited her a hell of a lot better than silk robes and too much makeup.

"Hey, girl!" Stephanie called. "Did you have a good trip?"

"Sure did." Katie nodded. "How about you? How was your day in hiding?"

"Good. We nailed down the details of the new base," she told Katie as they walked up the stairs. "We are getting the old building cleaned up to move into, and have already set the details to start pouring concrete for the new part tomorrow."

"Damn." Katie stifled a yawn. "That was fast."

"I know, but we really want to get out of this rubble and into the new place." Stephanie smiled. "Oh, and I am having an event at the old house tomorrow, for the transfer of the deeds. Will you come? You'll get to see some of the girls. They've been dying to see you."

"Absolutely." Katie smiled back and walked into the main area. "I wouldn't miss it for the world."

"Great!" Stephanie gave her a hug. "I will see you in the morning."

"Night." Katie watched as Stephanie headed to her room.

She walked the other way and breathed a sigh of relief when she walked into her bedroom.

It was good to be home; she had missed her bedroom. She put down her luggage and didn't even unpack, heading directly into the bathroom and turning on the water. She stripped and stepped into the deluge as soon as it got hot.

The water rushed over her, and she felt the aches and pains from the day washing down the drain. She had worked hard almost every day since she had been Damned, and this day had been no different.

She had managed, with the help of Damian, to save fifty souls, including an injured cop and about twelve children —not to mention that the thieves had been arrested and were being charged with a slew of things.

Those dickheads wouldn't see the light of day for a very long time.

When she was done showering, Katie threw on a set of yellow pajamas and headed to bed, super-excited to get comfy under the blankets and just straight pass out.

She climbed in and nestled down, laying her face on the pillow with a small smile playing across her lips.

The fabric was cool, soft, and smooth under her. She had initially been upset not to stay in the lush hotel, but when she got home and saw her bed, she had felt better about it. Katie had grown accustomed to her space; it now felt like home.

She only hoped that the new facility would be the same way, and that she could feel comfortable right away.

Slowly she closed her eyes, moaning in joy as she wrapped the blanket around her body. She laid that way for a moment, then turned to the other side, smiling again as she pulled the covers back around her.

About three minutes passed and she rolled again…and again…and again, until there was no smile on her face anymore. After about twenty minutes, she sat straight up and slammed the covers down. She huffed and puffed, trying to control her anger, but she was *livid*…and Pandora was the target of her fury.

GOD DAMN IT, PANDORA, she squealed in her mind. *There is so much sugar racing through my body right now that there is no way that I can go to fucking sleep!*

Uh, sorry. Pandora giggled, and there was absolutely no remorse in her tone. *I was hungry.*

No, you were not *hungry. You had a* craving, Katie argued. *If you had been hungry you would have told me so, not scarfed down the last of the fucking donuts. You just couldn't wait until the morning, could you?*

Hey, you are the one who has to physically put them in your mouth, she argued back. *So don't be all yelling 'Pandora made me do it.'*

Because you wouldn't shut up with your whining, Katie shot back. *Whatever. Fine! Fuck it, I guess I'm up.*

Katie rolled out of her bed and headed out to the living room, where she turned on the lights and plopped down sideways in the chair. She huffed as she grabbed the remote, feeling more than irritated that she wasn't drifting through dreamland; getting some rest like a normal person could.

She clicked on the recordings and started her soap, figuring it was as good a time as any to catch up on her shows. Of course Pandora was all about it, but Katie ignored her, too pissed to be friends with her at that moment.

A few minutes into the show, she heard a noise and looked over her shoulder. Eric shuffled out of his room. He nodded and headed into the kitchen to grab a soda, and returned to sink down on the couch. Katie smiled, figuring he was in the same position; couldn't sleep.

"At least I have something to do out here instead of staring at the walls," he told her. "I have to say though, it's not the same without Jeremy."

"Yeah." She sighed. "He would have flipped when he saw what happened on the last three episodes."

"And told us how ridiculous a portal to an alternate universe in the middle of Portland was." Eric laughed.

"I think it's legit." Katie giggled. "I mean, we fight demons from hell, which makes a portal not seem that crazy since I literally ran my car into one just a few weeks ago."

"Holy shit," Eric exclaimed, sitting up. "I didn't even think about that. Your life is mirroring theirs."

"Uh, or vice versa, except I don't have shirtless men all over the place and millions of dollars," Katie pointed out.

A few minutes after that Calvin, Stephanie, and Damian popped their heads out, rubbing their eyes, and they all gathered in the living room. Stephanie was very well versed on the show and quickly got Calvin back up to speed, since he had missed quite a few shows. Damian tried but ended up going back to his room, not at all interested.

Katie didn't blame him. He wasn't your typical soaps fiend.

Damian read philosophy books and painted. He didn't spend hours watching terrible acting and worse story lines. Katie, on the other hand, felt like she deserved some pointless television drama to numb her mind after everything she went through on a daily basis.

"I go to my room, and what happens? You fools start the show without me," Derek complained, jumping over the back of the couch to land between Stephanie and Eric. "Did you see what happened last show?"

"Yes," Katie said, gawking at his maneuver. "Alissa fell in love with the alien, but he had to leave her to go back to his planet. I mean, come on! This girl gets the short end of the love stick every time she turns around. She lives with a constant broken heart. It's bullshit, how they treat her on there."

"I know, right?" Eric agreed. "She is hot, and sweet too. One of these dudes needs to stop fucking with the hot-mess girls and scoop her up. I seriously think they are just all douchebag fuck-boys. Maybe she would have been better off going with the alien."

"That's what I was thinking," Stephanie remarked. "But it wasn't even a choice. He ghosted her, too. I bet he doesn't even *have* a mother; he was like born from a pod, or something."

"Men!" Katie shook her head. "You can't live with them, without them, or even a solar system away from them."

"*Amen,* sister!" Stephanie winked at her.

This team seriously had the strangest bonding routine ever.

While the other teams went on raids together, played ball together, and had dinner together every night, Korbin's Killers crowded around the television in the middle of the night and watched soap operas.

It was ridiculous, but Katie loved it. She couldn't help but wonder if that was the reason they had all become so close. They bonded over stupid shit, which made the big stuff that much more exciting. It might not teach them anything physically, but they felt comfortable enough to be soap opera whores together.

Soap-opera whores...bwahahahahahaha! And you said "love stick" earlier.

Pandora, shut the hell up and watch the show.

Stephanie walked through her old house, making sure that all the renovations she'd had done had turned out just right. The people taking over might know what the house had been, but since it was a charitable institution now she wanted to get rid of any remnants that might have been left from her former life.

She was in an odd position. Since she hadn't been infected in public and no one knew except their team, she wasn't "dead." She could still own property, still had a driver's license and a car...all the things her fellow demon hunters couldn't have—at least not without using Katie's solution. Her eyes didn't even have a red ring most of the time, since her demon wasn't very active and she herself was usually calm. *Usually.* But she had made her choice, and would start shedding the things that tied her to her old life…beginning today.

This was Mamacita's swan song. That role had been her survival for so long; her sanctuary, and protection from the life that she had run from. She had spent so much time being happy she didn't have to live that way anymore that she forgot she had put herself in a very similar situation by starting a whorehouse.

Korbin and the Killers had pulled her out of that mindset.

They had walked in when she had nothing else in her life, and offered her and the girls a sanctuary. It had taken her a long time to get used to the idea of trusting them, but when they had shown her they were there for them no matter what, she had started to have a tiny bit more faith in humanity.

She wouldn't wish the way she had grown up on anyone in the world, but as a Damned, those skills were coming in handy. They were being used to do good things, not bad, like the ones the cult had taught its followers when she was a child.

She turned a corner to find Damian standing in front of her, smiling broadly and looking nice in a suit and tie. He leaned toward Stephanie and hugged her tightly, thanking her for being so generous.

"Oh, it was nothing," she replied, patting him on the back. "It was time to move forward, so I needed to do this."

"Well, when you decided to pass the house to members of my church, the light shone on you." He smiled. "I'm just glad I could confirm that two of the young ladies previously under your care have been given a job here."

"I am so thankful for that." Stephanie looked around at the people in the house. "Those girls are very important to me, and they have been helped more by you, Korbin, and the rest than anyone else in their lives. They now feel like they have a future, for the first time."

"And how about you?" Damian asked.

"Oh, I'm still getting used to this life change." She chuckled. "My demon is quiet; rarely says anything and doesn't interrupt my thoughts, which I appreciate. When necessary, she gives me a boost. She is still terrified of Katie's demon, though, and I wish I knew why."

"Katie's demon can be a bit temperamental." Damian smiled. "And she is extremely powerful."

"I see." Stephanie looked up as the doorbell rang. "Well, let's get this party started."

"Yes," Damian agreed. "And put the past in the past. I will look in from time to time to make sure that everything is going well with the halfway house. I just want you to look forward."

"Thank you." Stephanie kissed Damian on the cheek. "You are a good friend."

Stephanie walked away, putting on the "Mamacita" face on one last time for the crowd.

They were there to wish the new owners good luck on their endeavor and fundraise for a profitable first year.

Katie and the team were there too, and even Korbin showed up later in the evening, looking deliciously suave in a three-piece suit.

They were there for their family, and even though the two older ladies taking over had no idea who or what they were, they felt like they could all be comfortable there. It was a big night for Stephanie; she got to say goodbye to her past life in a way they all wished they'd had the opportunity to.

It was a very bittersweet goodbye.

9

Korbin sat at his desk. He was going through the drawers to make some space and get rid of all the old stuff so he could move to the new place without such an immense amount of clutter.

He usually kept all the paperwork, filing it away just in case the higher-ups needed it. There was no reason to take everything old over there; it would be wasteful and useless. He tossed a pile into the shred box and raised his hands over his head.

He looked around the room, remembering when they first had turned the place into their base. He was going to miss it, but he knew that the new compound was going to fit them much better. He had just reached forward to continue when the phone rang.

"This is Korbin."

"Korbin, it's John William Smith from New York," a gruff voice replied.

"John, how are you?" Korbin asked. "What can I do for you? Are the weapons working out okay?"

"Oh, yeah." He chuckled. "Everyone is jealous. I'm pretty sure that when you start taking orders you will have more than your fair share. But that isn't why I was calling. My team heavy brought in a Damned yesterday while I was gone. She is freshly Damned and a bit wild, even for the Wyld Jokers. I can't integrate her right now."

"All right." Korbin leaned back. "What can I do for you?"

"Well, I was wondering if you could integrate her. You know, get her trained and teach her how everything works, and when I can take her you'll send her back to me?" he asked. "She is frisky, but with her kind of spirit she will fit in perfectly with us. I just don't have a spot for her this minute. You guys are short one person, right?"

"No, I'm not short. I picked up a woman just recently," Korbin replied. "But yes, send her. I'm sure she will be of use, with all the chaos going on. We can get her trained up perfectly for you. I mean, I have two ladies on this team already. Why not make it three?"

"Right?" John laughed. "Before long we are going to be calling you 'Korbin's Ladies.'"

"I might go crazy." Korbin chuckled. "Was she a coven find, or an innocent bystander?"

"I don't know if I would call her innocent." He sighed. "But no, she didn't ask to be Damned. There was another infected there, trying to get my heavy to make a deal to give him info on the teams. Melvin ended up killing her, and right when that happened Ella came walking out of the store, trash in hand. The demon jumped right into her. It was a shame, really. The demon is powerful, and quite strong-minded. The girl, though…she is tough as nails, has a strong personality, and doesn't understand at all why she is here. We gave her the options per SOP, but she hasn't really made a choice yet…not that being a guinea pig is a choice anyone would make. She needs a firm hand, but also someone who can show her what it's like to be part of a family and a team. She really doesn't have any experience in a family environment."

"A loner," Korbin confirmed. "Young?"

"Early twenties," John replied. "Still lived at home, doesn't care that they will think she is dead, didn't really have any attachments at all except to her parties and alcohol. Even those she did to stay away from her family and just do her thing. Like I said, doesn't like authority."

"You *didn't* say that." Korbin laughed. "But I figured it out when you told me she had no ties and hated her family. I think she will be fine here, and really, she isn't going to want her other two options, so knowing that might straighten her up a bit."

"Thanks, Korbin, I really appreciate it," John said gratefully.

"No problem, John. We'll fly out to you to pick her up," Korbin replied. They said their goodbyes, and he hung up the phone.

Korbin thought about bringing another person into the group. He had never liked fostering a Damned and then sending them away. It was like giving up one of your own, but he at least knew that would be the outcome.

If anyone could put a smartass in her place, it was him and his team. He thought about Katie, and what things had been like when she'd first gotten there. She hadn't been hard to get along with and didn't rebel, but she had been green and didn't want to be. He felt kind of bad for the way he had treated her, though. He had pretty much thrown her to the guys and let them deal with her.

In fact, he had been kind of an ass when she was coming through. For her it had worked out, but he knew that wouldn't be true for everyone.

This new girl would upset the balance just a bit, but maybe that was what they needed to get everyone back on track. Upset the flow of things, so everyone had to stop and look at themselves for a moment. Sometimes his Killers got complacent, thinking that training was just to get stronger, thinking that bonding was just to produce a nice home situation, but in reality it was all much more than that.

Training was to improve: get faster, understand your target, and get to know your enemy—the demon inside you. Bonding was great for quality of life, but it also was one of the main factors that kept you alive on those crazy incursions. You looked out for each other, because you knew what it would feel like to lose one of your teammates.

Either way, the girl was coming, and there was nothing any of them could do but buckle down and help. They had always been good at that, but they also never had someone like they described Ella to be. All Korbin could do was hope they were on top of this, like they had been when Katie arrived. He picked up his phone and texted Stephanie and Katie, asking them to head down to his office. He figured it might help if he had his two females pick her up instead of surrounding her with more men.

"Hey," Stephanie said, walking through the door. "Katie'll be here. She was finishing her food."

"How's the compound coming?"

"It's getting there." Stephanie smiled. "It'll be home sweet home in no time."

"Hey, boss!" Katie ran into the room with food on her face. "Sorry, I was hungry."

"It's okay." Korbin chuckled. "Have a seat. I have a mission for you."

"Nice!" Katie exclaimed. "Whose head are we smashing?"

"No one's, hopefully," he replied. "No, you are going to go to New York to pick up a new Damned on the company jet. She will be training with us, and then end up back in New York to work on that team. They needed some help getting things together, so I am stepping up."

Stephanie smirked. "You mean *we* are stepping up."

"Yes, *we*." He used his finger to form a circle. "As a team. Anyway, Damian normally handles these things, but he is unable to go. He has church in the morning, and not just at the chapel—at a larger church in Vegas. The new member is also a girl, so I figured it might be better to send you two than to send the guys."

"Poor thing." Stephanie frowned. "She must be so scared."

"Yeah, well…" Korbin chuckled, then cleared his throat. "From what I've been told, she isn't scared of much. She's a bit of a wild card, so you might be surprised at what you find."

"Oh, don't worry about that," Katie said, pushing up her sleeves. "I like a challenge."

"Yeah," Korbin replied. "I was afraid of that."

"When they said this thing is nice, I didn't know they meant ready-for-Hollywood nice," Stephanie said, running her hands over the leather chair arms in the jet.

"Yeah." Katie scoffed. "The first time I was on this thing, I felt like a damn Kardashian. Of course, on the way back I felt and looked more like Carrie covered in pig's blood, but still… The seats were comfortable."

"Maybe we can convince old stick-in-the-mud to let us take a vacation in this thing." Stephanie smiled.

"Mmmhmm, and maybe he will smile occasionally, too." Katie laughed, looking out the window as the plane made its descent into New York.

When they landed, the plane taxied to a private hanger and the doors closed right behind the plane.

Katie and Stephanie climbed off, finding John William, and the new not-so-bright-and-shining team member waiting for them. Stephanie introduced herself, and stepped to the side to try to talk to Ella. Katie smiled kindly at John and shook his hand firmly. The girl was a petulant twenty-year-old who didn't look the least bit happy about the entire situation.

"Ella." John gestured to Katie and Stephanie. "Meet your new team members. They are going to help you get straight, so you're ready to come back here and kick some ass."

"Great! First I start with Captain-fucking-America, and now I'm being passed over to Wonder Woman and She-

Ra." Ella snickered. "I already had enough shit going on in my life. This is not what I need or want. Just let me go back home, dammit."

"Well, I can see this one is grateful for still being alive." Stephanie sighed and reached out to Ella. "Come on, let's get you on the plane."

"Screw you!" Ella snatched her arm away. "I don't have to go anywhere with anyone."

"It's that, or I cut your head off right here." Stephanie pulled out her knife. "Your choice."

"You are a sick bitch." Ella folded her arms indignantly.

"Come on," Stephanie repeated, grabbing her by the ear and pulling her to the plane. "I want to get home."

Katie just watched, trying to hold back a laugh as Stephanie led Ella onto the jet by her ear. It was something her own mother would have done when she was a kid. Katie sighed and turned back to John.

"Sorry I'm handing you a mess." He ran a hand over his face in exasperation before holding it out to Katie. "I'm John, the leader of the Wyld Jokers."

"Katie." She shook his hand again. "We've heard the stories about New York."

"I'm sure." He chuckled. "You own the company, don't you?"

Katie pursed her lips and looked around, then leaned in and whispered, "Isn't the first rule of the company that we don't *mention* the company?"

Katie patted her blades and lifted her eyebrows, straightening up. He raised an eyebrow and looked down at his knives. Katie noticed that he had picked the ones with silvery handles, just like she would have. They were good knives.

"You like them?" She found herself unable to refrain from asking at least one question.

"They are freaking awesome," he told her. "I haven't really had a chance to use them yet with so much going on, but I plan on going out tonight and giving them some real-world experience. It's a good thing you have here, and I want you to know I have your back when it comes to the government. Secret kept one hundred percent. I'll remember the rule next time, too."

He chuckled, his square chin and deep dimples sticking in her mind. Katie smiled and patted her hands together awkwardly, looking around the hangar bay. She knew she should be more sociable, but it really wasn't her thing. He looked frustrated and gazed down at his feet, and Katie wondered if he was talking to his demon.

"So, next time you are in New York, let me take you out, all right?" he asked. "Las Vegas has lights, and we have action."

"That would be nice." Katie smiled. "I can see some New York-style demon-slaying in action."

Pandora laughed. *Hey stupid, I think he meant on a date.*

"Or just to dinner." Katie blushed.

"Or we could do both." He laughed, now more at ease.

He continued talking about the places he loved in New York, and his time in Las Vegas. Katie tried to pay attention, but she really had no desire to hear it. She just wanted to get back home, and on top of that, Pandora had started spouting shit again like she was a bitch in heat.

That man is scrumptious as hell, Pandora rambled. *I mean, look at those muscles! He's a bit older than I normally go for, but what the fuck. I'm not getting any younger.*

You're not HELping, Katie sang in her head.

Hell, I think I saw bats flying out of your rosey posey just the other day.

Can we NOT discuss my vagina right now?

I bet I could fit at least half a dozen donuts on his dick, and I'd eat them all while I...

FOR THE LOVE OF GOD, Katie mentally shouted, trying not to roll her eyes in front of John. You are aware that it wouldn't be you doing this, right? You're in MY body! Besides, this man is not my type.

No man is your type. Pandora scoffed. Why do you think I have a problem in here? No action, no flirting, no foreplay... No play, period. It's like living in a nunnery.

I like men just fine, Katie countered. I just don't need them like you do.

I DO NOT need men, Pandora snapped. I just like to have them around. What is so wrong with liking pleasure, huh? And don't give me some religious bullshit about it, either.

Nothing is wrong with it in moderation, Katie replied. But you are like a succubus.

I am nothing like those dim-witted idiots. She sniffed. Mere shadows.

Is that why you keep going on about how donuts are the perfect design? Katie asked. So, you can slide them on?

No, though it does sound like something I would say, Pandora replied. And I am really impressed that you thought that highly of me. Donuts are the perfect food, though, and they have the perfect shape, so it wouldn't be that far off to really get things done. You know, make it fun for a change, instead of so heavy and deep. Humans take sex way too seriously. Just get it in, get yours, and move on.

Wow, you are so romantic, Katie exclaimed.

That's what I'm talking about, Pandora replied. *Leave romance for the dinner. Sex should be fun and exciting.*

You are *a demon,* Katie mused. *I guess you don't get romanced often enough to appreciate the importance of it.*

Maybe not, Pandora replied. *But I do know that in my very long time in existence, I have only met one man who truly gave two shits about romance. It's for the girls, to make us want to open our legs. I am sure some man created romance a long time ago to make it easier to get in a girl's hooha.*

Katie looked at John and said her goodbyes, needing to get herself out of the situation fast before Pandora blew up inside her, leaving the walls of her mind soaking with the explosion of her pent-up desires.

When she climbed back onto the plane, Stephanie was sitting in her chair calmly reading a magazine while Ella cursed and groaned, rubbing the side of her head.

She was going to be an interesting one to train.

atie sat quietly on her bed reading a book, her mind going in and out of the most recent events. She still was struggling with losing a teammate, and on top of that she wanted to kill T'Chezz for taking her precious baby—her car. She looked up when there was a knock on the door, putting her bookmark in and walking over to open it.

"Hey there, priest guy." Katie smiled at Damian. "What can I do for you?"

"I was wondering if you could come over and speak with Ella," Damian requested. "We are having our fair share of issues with her. She is not very happy to be in this position, and Stephanie seems to believe the only solution is 'a firm hand for a lazy child.' I am thinking there might be another way."

Katie laughed, imagining Stephanie shaking her finger at Ella. She nodded and tossed her book back on the bed, closing her bedroom door and following Damian downstairs to the examination room.

When she entered Ella was telling Stephanie off, and Stephanie looked like she might just attempt to take Ella over her knee and beat the shit out of her ass. They both stopped and looked at Katie.

"Oh, great! Let me guess…you are the good cop," Ella growled.

"Uh, I don't think anyone has ever called me that before." Katie laughed and glanced at Damian, who was chuckling under his breath. "Maybe a cop, but never the good one. I just came to see what the hell this was all about. I could hear you yelling all the way down the hall."

"This is bullshit! Just take the thing out of me and let it go," Ella snarled, pouting.

"Folks?" Katie looked at Stephanie and Damian. "Could you give us a second?"

"Be my guest." Stephanie waved and walked out of the room.

Damian smiled and winked as he left, shutting the door behind him.

Katie turned back to Ella and watched her body language. Her hands were pressed together nervously, her eyes were on the floor, and her cheeks were bright red. There was something more going on than just being pissed at the situation.

"What did you do back in the City?"

"I worked at Starbucks," she mumbled.

"That's cool, though I would rather get my coffee from someone small and local." Katie shrugged.

"I know, right?" Ella agreed, looking up at her. "Those

yuppies come in and out all day and all they want to do is 'recycle, reuse, rescue,' and whatever else they can come up with, but they buy from a multinational corporation that bleeds the environment dry."

"It's gross." Katie shook her head. "So, any good friends? Boyfriend, maybe?"

"No." Ella shrugged. "Just my parents. I can't believe I am saying this, but I actually miss them. I mean, I know I can't see them again, but I don't want it to *be* that way."

"I had a really hard time with that as well," Katie told her. "I had a mom who loved me to death, and friends. I was in college. I had a hard time even thinking about letting that all go. I guess when you are left with no other choice, you just kind of do it."

"What did you do?" Ella asked.

"Well, at first, nothing," Katie admitted, leaning against the examination table. "Until my demon confessed that she was locking down some of my emotions because they were too much trouble to deal with. After that I was able to get them out, you know? I was able to grieve the losses. It was strange to know that I was the dead one, but I was missing my family and friends like they had died. I guess I missed them for missing me. It was really rough. I really thought I was tough-skinned until I came here and broke down until I was pretty much a shell. But then I built myself back up, with the help and support of my team."

"Did it take long?" Ella wondered.

"No." Katie tilted her head and looked at Ella. "But mostly because I didn't *have* long. I was called out on my first incursion just a couple days after I got here. I had to toughen up or die. The first step for you, though? You need to cry. I know it sounds stupid and hokey, but everyone here," she waved a hand in the general direction of the building, "the guys and girls, they have gone through that. Once you let the emotional part out, you will be able to come to terms with what has happened to you. It's not easy, I won't lie. You go from your normal life to being this capsule for evil, but you're being asked to do good with it. Meanwhile, everyone else in your life has disappeared."

"What happens when you've come to terms with it?" Ella asked.

"Well, then you get some awesome training," she enthused. "Play with some really cool toys and then kick monster ass like you are in the movies, hopefully without dying. If possible, during all that you want to try to have a relationship of sorts with your demon. It won't do you any good to fight it, although you don't want to release yourself to it, and they can give you some valuable assistance that can help you survive. My demon helps me all the time, but most of the time I keep it to myself. Sometimes, though, she helps me with something so huge that it gets covered up so people—even the other teams—won't get freaked out."

"I'm scared to talk to him," Ella admitted.

"Don't be. At this point, you hold all the cards," Katie advised. "You are in control of the situation. You know what? I have an idea. Hold on one second…let me talk to my demon."

Do you think you could communicate with her demon? Katie asked.

I can sense that this one is a big motherfucker. Pandora sniffed. *I'll do it, but I want something in return.*

Okay. Katie sighed. *Like what? A year's supply of donuts? All the Italian you can eat?*

Nothing like that, Pandora chirped mischievously. *I want another car.*

Oh, lord, Katie moaned.

And not just any car, one just like the one you had, Pandora explained. *I really enjoyed riding around in that thing, top down, the sun on your back. Just cruising. That is, until Ding-a-ling Demon showed up and ruined everything.*

And if I promise you we will look for another vehicle—no promises on the type—you will talk to Ella's demon? Katie asked. *The girl is having a really hard time with this change. and I think if the demon will talk to her she will feel more comfortable with the whole thing. Right now she is terrified, and that is going to get her killed fast.*

Yes, I will talk to him, Pandora assured her.

All right, Katie agreed. *Another vehicle coming up...sometime.*

Katie took a deep breath and sat down in the chair, leaning back and closing her eyes. Pandora would take over her vocal cords, which was a very strange feeling.

Pandora was preparing to contact Ella's demon; she could tell because there was a sense of concern that Katie did not typically feel. She thought about asking her what was up, but she figured it was best that she just let her do her thing.

She didn't need a distraction.

"Melneck?" Pandora spoke through Katie's mouth. "I

thought your scent seemed familiar. Why are you hiding in there?"

"Small world." Melneck scoffed, speaking through Ella and scaring the hell out of her. "Oh, sit still, child. It's not that bad," he told the girl.

"She's new. Give her some space," Pandora advised.

"Since when did you become sympathetic to the human plight?" he asked.

"Not really sympathetic, but it's easier if they calm the hell down," she told him. "What are you doing here, anyway?"

"Shouldn't I ask *you* that?" he asked. "Never expected to see someone from the Eight slumming up here."

"I was tricked by my asshole brother-from-another-mother," Pandora growled. "He tried to get me out of the picture and into a form he can kill easier. At least he thought he could kill me easier, but that doesn't seem to be how things are working out for him. Silly demon…always thinking he can one-up me, never thinking about the fact that I am fucking smarter than him most of the time, and way older."

"Well, I guess that makes two of us, then," Melneck replied.

"What do you mean?" Pandora asked. "What does T'Chezz have to do with you and this girl?"

"Nothing to do with the girl," he assured her, "but I came here under orders from T'Chezz as a final payment for a favor I owed him."

"Bet you'll think twice next time about asking for a favor from that jackass." Pandora scoffed.

"Yeah, never again," he agreed. "I heard someone

speaking to my previous host's dead body after I switched over to this kid. They told it, 'Seems like I won't have to kill you after all. T'Chezz will be *happy*.' She was being moved to a blacked-out SUV when it happened. I couldn't see who it was since my human had completely collapsed, but I could tell the sniveling voice was someone from below."

"That does not surprise me at all." Pandora chuckled. "I think T'Chezz underestimates the power we have in our human hosts. I also think that he was trying to do that to me, or rather *still* trying. He doesn't want me in the picture. He knows that his demons would follow me in a heartbeat, though I don't really want to be a leader. I don't see what he would get out of killing you, but he never did make much sense with that shit."

"Well, either way, I know he wants me dead," Melneck agreed. "He sent someone up to follow me around and then kill me off as soon as I was done. It serves T'Chezz right that his effort failed to turn a Damned, anyway. He has very little faith in humankind, that's for sure. He believes them to be a lot weaker than they really are, and it's a shame. I'm not saying I'm on their side—I'm on *my* side—but they could give him quite a fight. He doesn't even realize it."

"I think he is starting to, if he is sending you up here to do his dirty work," Pandora suggested.

"I don't really know why he thinks it would matter if I went back to hell?" Melneck mused. "It's not like I'm not headed back there anyway."

"Yeah, but this is a little different," Pandora told him. "I know the demon you are talking about, and when he kills, you either go way down into the depths of the fire not to resurface for centuries, or maybe to a true death."

"A true death?" Melneck paused a moment. "I thought that was a myth."

"Not a myth." Pandora shuddered. "I've seen it. Demons can have a true death, their souls completely extinguished and their bodies turned to dust. There is no coming back from that. I am not sure how that happens yet, but I am *not* willing to test it. I might get bored down there in hell, but I'm not looking to completely disappear."

"This is bullshit," Melneck yelled angrily, raising his human to her feet and forcing her to pace. "Seriously, this is complete and utter crap. I had plans, and now every one of them is going to have to be put on hold. Talk about annoying! This is the epitome of it."

"At least you're still alive." Pandora shrugged Katie's shoulders. "Anyway, just try to help your human out. Think of it this way: the stronger she is, the longer *you* live. If she dies, you die. When it's time you can get free and go back, but right now this might be the safest place for you. They think you are dead, but that doesn't mean they won't try to kill your human. Lay low for a while; build something with her and make her more confident. You'll get your moment."

Pandora released Katie's vocal cords and Katie rubbed her throat. She looked at Ella, who had stopped pacing and was doing the same thing with a look of terror in her eyes. She forgot to prepare her for that, but she seemed to have taken it at least somewhat well.

"Sorry, forgot to tell you that part." Katie smiled.

"Yeah." Ella shook her head.

Her demon is named Melneck, Pandora explained to Katie. He is one of the tightest-assed demons I have ever met. I knew him down below, and seriously...if he ate coal, diamonds would come out when he took a shit.

That is disgusting.

No one down there likes him, because he is a presumptuous ass, Pandora replied. The good news though is that he found out T'Chezz was planning his death, so he isn't loyal to anyone but himself right now. I told him to help Ella; that the more he helped her, the longer both of them would stay alive. I am pretty sure he agreed, and I don't think she will struggle too much with it.

Good work, Katie told her.

"Ella," Katie began, moving back over to the girl, "I need you to start working through your feelings. We are all a family here. We've all been through the process, and we are all here to help you with anything that you need. There are also counselors on the team, if you'd prefer one of those. However, after talking with Korbin and Damian, we know that your priority is to begin training. Training is one of the most important things we do, and it's not just for workouts and tiny waistlines. It's for survival, because right now you are weak, so you run the risk of dying permanently."

"I don't want to die," Ella said quietly. "I know I said that in New York, but I didn't mean it."

"It's okay." Katie smiled. "We all go through a really rough time when things start to change. How about we forget about the past and start fresh right here in this glass-boxed room? You can embrace your new situation and learn to do the things we do."

"Okay," Ella agreed, although she wasn't very happy about it.

"Perfect!" Katie stood up and headed for the door. "We start training at six, so get some sleep tonight and be ready by that time to set things on fire."

"Okay," Ella replied as Katie left the room.

That's not so bad, Ella thought. *Six in the evening is not a bad time to start.*

L*ook, you little bitch,* Melneck hissed. *Get your non-athletic funky ass out of this bed. I am not here to be your goddamned babysitter.*

Dream on, asshole. Ella laughed mentally. *My parents spent twenty years trying to get me to do what they wanted. You think you are any better? Fucking think again. I don't get up before the crack of noon on an early day.*

Melneck growled and ran his powers through her body, fucking with her intestines. She immediately became very gaseous, stinking up the entire room. She didn't budge, just pulled her covers tighter around her. She did not want to get up, she did not want to train, and she did not want to deal with the rest of this team of soldier do-gooders. She wanted to stay in bed and decide later if training was something she wanted to do. She wasn't about to start running, doing pushups, and fencing without fully feeling into it. Melneck increased the pressure on her intestines.

I really feel like you are hurting yourself more than me.

Melneck chuckled. *I have smelled sulphur in one form or another my whole life, so this is like a sweet memory from my parents' house. It's like I am getting ready to start my day.*

You think it's pleasant now, wait until you see what I can do to your body, Melneck growled. *Don't like your thighs? I can make them fatter. Your ass too big? You haven't seen nothing yet. Oh yeah, then there is my favorite...acne.*

You don't scare me, Ella snarled.

IF YOU DON'T GET YOUR GIANT ASS OUT OF THIS BED, YOU WILL GET DIARRHEA NEXT, Melneck screamed. *I am not going to put up with some lazy piece of shit. I will take over your body. Don't fucking test me girl!*

"YOU ARE SUCH AN ASSHOLE!" Ella screamed out loud, throwing the covers back. "I swear, when I get you out of me I am going to kill you myself."

I'd like to see you get so strong that a threat like that would worry me in the least. He chuckled. *Right now, all I would have to do is flick you and you would break in half. Now get up. Take a shower, brush you goddamn teeth because your breath smells like a demon's rotten asshole, and get downstairs. I'm sure they are all waiting for you.*

Oh joy, Ella growled, getting out of the bed. *A new happy little family, just waiting to meet their new fucking pet. Not what I signed up for. I'd rather work non-stop shifts at Starbucks with the same obnoxious bitch ordering the same obnoxious fucking drink with fifty-seven ingredients. And to think I used to think that was the absolute description of hell! Who would have thought I would have found the real hell in a desert?*

Oh, trust me honey, you've seen nothing yet if you think this is hell. Melneck laughed.

"There she is," Katie told Calvin. "Good luck with her."

"I grew up in the ghetto." He cracked his knuckles. "This girl has nothing on me."

"Right." Katie chuckled, waving to him as she walked away.

"Good morning, Ella," Calvin said as he walked up to her. "I am your team leader Calvin. I'm second in charge under Korbin, who you will meet eventually. I want to start out the day with some questions."

"Oh, I *love* questions," Ella grumbled, walking over to the table with Calvin. "Why is this place such a wreck?"

"We had a demon invasion here," he replied. "We got them all, but it was tough on the structure. So, tell me about yourself. Where did you come from, what are your interests, and so on?"

"Well, I am not really interested in anything," she said pointedly. "I was a straight-A student in high school, but not because I cared to study—just because it was so damn easy. They tried to challenge me with AP classes, but they were all yawnworthy. All they included was more homework. The other crap was already in my head."

"Okay." Calvin wrote some notes. "You sound like a very smart young lady. What did you do before you got infected?"

"I worked at Starbucks. That's about it."

"No college?" he asked.

"I got a couple scholarships." She shrugged, looking around. "But I wasn't interested. My parents just couldn't wrap their little heads around that. College wasn't for me.

They saw opportunity; for me, all it included was learning more and 'getting ahead,' and I have no idea what that means."

"What did you *want* to do?" Calvin asked.

"I dunno." She shrugged. "I only have one life, so I want to enjoy it. I didn't want to become a slave, to be a tool for the government for forty-five years just so I could retire when I was too old to enjoy myself. Hell, no! There is too much in this world for me to experience. I am doing that shit now while I'm young, while I can go out and see the world without a walker and a bunch of pills to keep me alive. We are born into slavery and we work our whole lives thinking it's for the greater purpose, but when we finally get to the end all we have to look back on is what we did at work. No, thanks."

Calvin nodded along, listening to what she was saying but not hearing anything new, for all she was so smart. Sure, she was probably genius-level, but that wasn't going to help her when she was facing down a six-hundred-pound demon with nothing but a sword and her talent. She didn't seem to understand why she was there or what she would be doing.

"Did you have any interests outside of school or work?"

"Parties. Smoking weed and chillin' out with my friends."

"Right." He looked up at her. "I meant like physical activities."

"Nope." She yawned.

"Nothing?" he asked. "No fighting, no wrestling… Maybe competitive volleyball?"

"Competitive volleyball?" She snickered, peering at him to see if he was trying to put one over on her.

He wasn't.

"Don't knock it," Calvin told her. "I've become a believer in the power of volleyball. Katie there…she is the team heavy, meaning she carries us in almost all the fights. When she came in here she had nothing under her belt except competitive volleyball, and she is the best ass-kicker on the team."

"Oh?" Ella lifted one eyebrow. "How nice for her."

"All right," Calvin said, putting down his notes. "I think at this point the best thing for us to do is just see what you have in you. Go put on some tennis shoes, I put some new ones on the bench, along with some workout clothes that Katie brought down. We'll hit the track."

Ella rolled her eyes and stood up to grab the clothes. This was not her idea of a fun time in the least. She changed and they went out to the track, starting off with a slow jog. She had no interest in proving herself to these goons, and she definitely wasn't going to break a sweat for any of them.

Come on, Melneck griped. *You have the stamina of a six-year-old.*

Shut up, Ella growled.

I'm not kidding, Melneck snapped. *I have seen a toad move faster than you. A big fat one, missing one leg, just skimming along at a quicker pace than this.*

Ella picked up her pace and scowled. She had to figure out how to deal with humans who wanted to work her harder than her parents had and a demon who was a complete and total asshole.

As she ran she thought about what had happened the day before. As if her day hadn't already had a hard enough beginning running from her mother, she'd had to walk the trash out at that specific moment, thinking she could sneak a smoke.

Oh, you won't be smoking anymore, Melneck told her. *Disgusting habit. I drained the nicotine from your system while you were asleep and made it so you were no longer addicted.*

Great, my demon is now an ad for Chantix. She scoffed.

I also healed your lungs, he added. *Which is why I am so surprised you move so slowly.*

Ella ignored him as she ran around the track, trying to focus enough to not trip over her feet. She seriously couldn't figure out how her life had gotten so much worse. She had enough shit in her life; she did *not* need this.

This is going to be sooo awesome, Melneck crowed excitedly. *Every day we will get up early and eat a healthy breakfast —egg whites, toast, and maybe some coffee if you're good—and then hit the gym. We have a whole gym at our fingertips. I will come up with a training routine for you. It will be fabulous.*

Great, thanks. She groaned. *I just want to go back to bed and get high. Maybe not in that order, but you fucking get it.*

Not anymore, sugar tits, Melneck cooed. *We are on the road to freedom here. Freedom from fat, cholesterol, and high sodium.*

"I really got to get out of here," she mumbled to herself as she made the turn.

Ella had gotten very tired of hearing Melneck, so she put

her ass into everything else she did during the rest of training. She even went in and ate dinner with the team, getting to know them a little.

She had to admit the whole thing had appeal, but it was *not* for her. By the time she made it back to her bedroom that night, she had created an entire plan to break free from the compound. She stood at her bed, twisting the sheets she found in the closet and tying them end to end.

She quietly opened her window and lowered the sheets to the ground, securing the other end to the leg of her bed. Slowly she crawled out the window and lowered herself to the ground, making sure to avoid the other glass panels in case someone was awake. She hit the ground with a thud on legs swollen and sore from the early workout. She was just about to make a run for it when she heard a whisper behind her.

"Where you are going?" the voice asked. "Where you are going? I left you a note…"

Ella slowly turned around, slightly nervous about who she would find. She could see two round red eyes staring back at her from the darkness. Her heart started to beat faster and she clapped her palms in front of her. She couldn't talk much less move by that point, and she was starting to think laps around the gym wouldn't be that bad after all.

"And the note says," the voice snarled as Stephanie stepped into the light, blinking the red from her eyes and clearing her throat, "get yourself back in that fucking bed or I will kick your ass so hard you will need to send notes to it via air mail!"

Ella let out a deep breath and relaxed her shoulders. She

hated that she had gotten caught, but she was thankful the red eyes were just Stephanie. She had thought for sure that she was a goner. She stiffened her face and rolled her eyes before turning and sulking toward the door.

"Nah ah ah," Stephanie cautioned, waving her finger. "You came out the window, so you will go back in through the window."

"What?" Ella looked at her in surprise. "I could fall!"

"Mmmhmm, yes," Stephanie said, looking at her nails. "You could, and I will be right here in the sand waiting for you to do it so I can laugh at your useless ass. Please start climbing, because I really want to watch that happen. It would seriously make my whole week."

"You are a sadistic *BITCH*," Ella growled. "If I fall I'm suing someone. I don't know who yet, but I will find someone, and I will take them the fuck down."

Ella walked over to the dangling sheet, looking up it to the open window. She sighed, grabbed the fabric, and put one foot on the wall. Holding tightly to the sheet rope, she slowly pulled herself up. She climbed a bit higher and looked down at Stephanie, who stood there with her hands on her hips and a smirk on her face.

"Fucking assholes," she mumbled. "They think they are so cute, with the lessons they want to teach me. All I see is a fucking rope that I have to climb. It could come loose at any point, and I could break my fucking legs."

When Ella got to the windowsill, she carefully grabbed the edge. She got a good hold on it and pulled herself toward the wall, but as soon as she got close her foot slipped, rocks crumbling beneath her. She let out a quiet yelp as she grabbed the sill with both hands and hung there, her arms shaking and nerves blowing up in her chest. Melneck pushed slightly, giving her the strength she needed to get through the window.

Why did you help me? she asked after she was in safely.

Failure would have affected your sleep schedule, he told her. *And we are on a very tight schedule.*

You, Ella said, pulling the sheet rope up from the ground, *are fucking insufferable.*

Oh, please. Melneck laughed. *Petulant child, I've been told that by beings who could gnaw on your longest bone like a toothpick. You telling me that just makes my heart feel warm. It's like you are complimenting me on a job well done, but I cannot say the same for you with your asinine fourteen-year-old's plan to escape. I thought you were a genius. Was that all you could come up with?*

I'm under a lot of pressure here, she griped, untying the sheets. *And I didn't hear you giving me any good pointers. You were too busy acting like Jane-fucking-Fonda coming up with a new workout routine. If you put Pilates or jazzercise or hip hop or anything like that on that list, I will kill myself just to spite you.*

Trust me, honey, no one wants to see you jumping around to hip hop, okay? Melneck chuckled. *You need help, and you don't have time to play around with some at-home workouts. What I got for you is going to tone, burn, and churn those muscles to perfection.*

Great, she grumbled. *This is my fucking life.*

Calvin laughed. "This girl is quite the handful." He was sitting in Korbin's office with Katie and Damian. "She hates what she is doing here, even though she really has no clue about the extent of it yet."

"I don't know if I would trust her with a weapon," Katie mused. "She's liable to stab herself or one of us by accident."

"Or on purpose." Calvin chuckled.

"Oh, I think she would show her true colors in action," Damian said. "We have to have a little more faith in her than that. We did for you, Katie, and you have become a badass."

Katie looked at Korbin as he picked up his ringing phone and walked from the room to take the call.

She sighed, thinking that Damian was right. When she'd gotten there she had been nothing but a volleyball player, and they turned her into a killer—though she still wasn't sure she would consider herself a badass.

Either way, Ella was confused and scared, and she needed all the positive reinforcement she could get. She didn't need people talking down to her, but she was just such a damn bitch all the time it was hard not to.

With that thought Korbin walked back in, shaking his head. He sat down in his chair and rubbed his face, pulling everyone's attention.

"What's going on, Korbin?" Calvin asked. "You look like you just have seen a ghost."

"Kind of," Korbin replied. "That was the National Military Advisor on the phone. He wants to see the facilities, since he heard that we took quite a bit of damage recently."

"Damn!" Calvin exclaimed. "Well, how much time do we have? We can start cleaning everything out right away."

"There won't be enough time for that," Korbin said. "He will be here in twenty-four hours."

"Shit!" Katie sat up straight. "That's one hell of a short notice."

"We need to get all the weapons out of here," Calvin suggested. "Not just the new ones, but everything that's not military issue."

"You're right," Korbin agreed. "Those weapons need to be taken over to the new base and stowed away. Calvin, I want you to grab Derek from upstairs, and the two of you will start loading everything into the truck. The new location is in the GPS, so take it over there and find a good spot for it. I think if you look on the blue prints you will find an armory on the property, so try there first."

"You got it, boss." Calvin stood up and jogged from the room.

"What about us?" Katie asked as Korbin picked up the phone, putting one finger up to silence her.

"Stephanie," Korbin said into the phone. "Something big just came up. I need you to come back home right away."

A squawk came out of the speaker.

"I really don't care about the sale at Nordstrom's," Korbin said flatly.

Loud cursing ensued.

"Right. Okay, see you soon."

Katie chuckled and glanced at Damian. Korbin hung up the phone and shook his head, running his hands through his hair.

"Why now?" he asked loudly. "Katie and Damian, I want you guys to get Ella packed up and take her back to New York to finish her training. It will be good for her to train in her home environment, and on top of that the New York team is asking for some help related to a spate of severe attacks in the area. I'm sure they will be happy to have you out there."

"What about here?" Katie asked. "New York is a long flight away."

"I know, but things have been really quiet around here," Korbin replied. "We haven't gotten any intel about this area lately. I will give them four days of your time to help out and get Ella trained before I want you back here to get everything moved over. This was probably a good thing in disguise, since we were dragging our feet getting over to the new location anyway.

"I do need you back in four days, though, so don't lollygag over there. Get your shit done, help them out, and come back home. But—do I even need to say this?—please try to keep Pandora from performing any of her more spectacular tricks in public. They still don't know what you two can do, and I don't believe this is the right time to let anyone else in on it."

Pandora snickered, and Katie shrugged. "As if I get a vote, but I *will* try. Normal demon-hunter shit only, check."

"Got it," Damian confirmed.

"Come on, Damian." Katie smirked. "We get to take your namesake back to New York and get her all tucked in with her new family."

"You're an ass," he said, following Katie out the door.

"Am I going to have to bring tissues?" she asked. "You know I don't deal well with men who cry. I just want to make sure you have something to blow your nose on."

"I hate you," he said pleasantly.

Katie laughed. "That is not nice, considering you are a man of the cloth."

"You sound like your demon." He chuckled.

Finally! Pandora squealed.

Stephanie parked her car and left her bags in the back grumbling to herself about missing out on one hell of a sale. She took the stairs to Korbin's office, stopping for a moment as Damian and Katie came down the hall. Damian was scowling and Katie was laughing, so she knew she was giving him shit about something.

"Hey, guys!" Stephanie smiled. "Anything I should be warned about?"

"He'll tell you." Damian shook his head. "It's always something, right?"

"Yeah." Stephanie nodded and continued down the hall.

She walked into the office and sat down, watching Korbin shuffle through paperwork and jam it angrily into the shredder. She lifted one eyebrow but let him finish, never having seen him in a tizzy before. When he was done, he straightened up and let out a huge puff of air. He looked at her and nodded.

"Sorry for pulling you from your shopping," he grumbled.

"Yeah, well, now you owe me a pair of Jimmy Choos." She smirked. "So what's up? You look like your head is going to explode."

"We need to get rid of as much evidence of Joshua's stuff and the business as we can in twenty-four hours," he told her. "What can you do with that?"

"Hmmm..." Stephanie leaned back in her chair, thinking.

She sat there for a few moments, rolling some ideas around in her head. There was a lot to get rid of, and unfortunately it was all too heavy just to load in the back of the truck and take off with. Plus, there was some serious ductwork involved with some of the equipment. She knew she would need professional help moving things, and on very short notice—which brought it down to the almighty dollar.

"How much do I have to work with here?" she asked.

Korbin gazed at her for a moment, then sat back and closed his eyes. She knew he had expected it to be done without money, but that just wasn't how the world worked. Even with the guys, it couldn't be done that fast. She needed professionals, and that meant a budget. Finally he leaned forward and blew out another large breath of air, rolling his eyes.

"I don't know. What can you do with fifty thousand?"

Stephanie didn't answer the question, just nodded and popped out of the chair to make her way out of the office. Korbin shut his eyes as the door closed behind her. He shook his head and turned back to his paperwork grumbling under his breath.

"That woman is inscrutable," he whispered to himself. "She is going to bleed me dry by the end of all of this. Nothing will go right, not a goddamned thing. Why can't it just be easy?"

He finished shredding the paperwork and picked up the phone, calling his contact at the airport. He had to put a short-notice trip to New York together for Katie, Damian, and Ella or they would never get out of Las Vegas in time. The last thing he needed was a smart-ass, a priest, and an unstable Damned floating around when the government arrived. He had enough headache on his plate as it was.

"Hey, it's Korbin," he began. "I need to put together a quick flight from here to New York, leaving in a couple of hours... No, it's not an emergency per se, I just need to get some of my people back there as soon as possible."

The guy put him on hold and transferred him to the pilot, where he explained it all over again. The pilot was a lot easier to work with, and pulled up all the information while they were on the phone. When that was done, he figured it was the perfect time to talk about choppers.

"I had a more personal question to ask," Korbin began.

"I want to find out about acquiring helicopters—or one helicopter—and I need you to tell me what kind would be best."

"Are we talking the kind that was used before, or a tourist helicopter?" the pilot asked.

"Not tourist," Korbin replied. "Something like what we used before, only this time we're not renting. I need to get a helicopter for full-time use, and probably hire maintenance technicians for it as well. Oh, and at least one pilot who would agree to be on short-notice call out of the Las Vegas area—a discreet pilot, preferably with combat experience, just in case we…uh…hit bad weather or something like that."

"Sometimes I think you are worse than our new trainee." Damian smiled. "You have gotten too big for your britches."

"Is that a fat joke?" Katie asked, looking back at her ass.

Damian rolled his eyes and held the door to the main living area open. The two of them entered and found Ella talking with Eric in the living room. She had an innocent look on her face, so Katie knew something was up. Eric was sinking into it, too—just like a man. Ella had him wrapped around her little finger so tightly he didn't even hear them come through the door.

"I know that Katie and Stephanie are girls," she cooed. "But I'm just not built for this, you know? I am fragile and sensitive. I shouldn't be forced to kill or be killed; it just isn't right. For a man like you it comes easy. You are strong and brave, but me? No way, I need to be in a gentler setting…maybe helping the poor or working with animals or something. Demon or not, I am not a bad person, and all this is just too much to deal with."

"I under—" Eric stopped and looked at Katie.

"Sorry to interrupt." Katie raised an eyebrow at Eric. "Ella, go get your stuff packed. We have to go back to New York."

"Really?" she said excitedly. "Oh my God, I have missed my family so much. I can't wait to get back home and have a good cup of coffee and just relax. My bed has been calling for me, for sure."

"Ella…" Katie stopped her before she could leave the room. "This isn't like that. You are Damned now, and unfortunately there is nothing you can do to change that. You were pronounced dead when that demon entered you, before you were taken away by John's team. You can't just show up at your parents' house. That is the way these things work. I know that's hard to understand, but you are going to your new base."

"You mean back with the freaks who did this to me in the first place?" she asked, irritated. "To the team that pushed me off on other people? I wasn't good enough for you, so now you are sending me back to them."

"You were always going back there," Katie reminded her, feeling badly for the girl. "We are going to work with you there."

"Whatever," she snapped. "This is all just more bullshit."

Ella stomped down the hallway and slammed her door, rattling the already-crooked pictures on the wall.

Katie looked at Damian, who sighed and rolled his eyes

before going to his room to pack. Katie shook her head and turned back to Eric. The man had a bewildered look on his face, as if he had no idea what had just happened. Katie calmed herself and walked over to sit down next to Eric, and looked at him with raised eyebrows.

"What?" he blurted.

"The female demon, otherwise known as 'Ella,' just took over your body," Katie told him. "Like, worse than the demon you already have inside you."

"What the hell?" He shook his head. "We were just talking. I mean, she was telling me about her life before this. She seemed so genuine…until a second ago. I would be mad too, but she doesn't get it, does she? Well, fuck."

He shook his head when he reached the correct conclusion.

"I got suckered, didn't I?" he asked, lowering his head.

"It's okay." Katie laughed. "It happens, but you are now a veteran here. You have to take a firm hand; don't allow the newbies to give you a sob story. We got lucky with you and Jeremy—and Stephanie, for that matter. You guys were all gung ho, ready to take on the worst of the worst. Even I didn't give them as much trouble as she has, but we are going to see it more than not and you need to be ready for it. You can't let them break your heart. You know there are no other options here."

Eric sighed. "She was really good at it."

"Yeah, I have a feeling that had nothing to do with the demon inside her." Katie looked down the hall. "I think she has been perfecting the art of sob stories for a very long time to get through life. She is super-smart and reads people very well, and she saw you as the perfect target. You aren't a leader, you have kind eyes, and you were ripe for the picking. It's really not your fault. She conned you like a guy cons a girl at a bar trying to get laid. She was trying to get you to free her from the invisible cage, but the thing is…she put herself in that cage. If she doesn't get with it, she is going to end up dead during an incursion."

"I mean, seriously?" Eric asked, looking Katie in the eyes. "What was I supposed to do in that situation? It has been scientifically proven that females have the ability to warp men's minds. It's biological; like, born and bred into you girls to do that to us."

"Well, you do have a point." Katie smiled and patted him on the arm. "You definitely have a point."

13

Katie looked out the plane's window after Ella had fallen asleep with her headphones in and music blaring. Damian was several seats back, working on a sermon for the next time he led a service at the church he had gotten involved with. There was a silence in the plane that she wasn't used to, and though she could have used a little extra shut eye, she wasn't tired— not in the least.

What do you think T'Chezz is doing right now? Katie asked Pandora. *Like, right in this moment in the fiery pits of hell.*

I dunno, Pandora grumped. *Probably torturing a soul or commanding his minions or taking a shit or something.*

You guys take shits? Katie asked.

No, she admitted, *but it was something a human would understand.*

I meant, what are his plans for the future? Katie rolled her eyes. *For us, for Earth, for the humans. Trying to figure out his next move is really our only choice right now, and you know him the best. We can't allow him to get his forces back together. I saw the size of his leg and I don't think I'm ready take it out, much less his whole body. Dude was huge! Unless you have any better ideas?*

I should have just taken care of him when I thought about it decades ago. Pandora sighed. *That would have been the simplest thing for me to do. I guess I could possibly work up some plans; something that would create a weapon that would destroy him.*

That's what I'm talkin' about, Katie exclaimed. *Let's think about how to end this, not just prolong the fight.*

You do realize that if I create a weapon that can destroy him, I will eventually be destroyed by it as well, Pandora pointed out. *I don't like the sound of that.*

We can all be destroyed, Pandora, Katie admitted. *At some point the question isn't whether it is demon versus human. It's about who are you closest to. It has to be who deserves to be here, not what species you are—if you can consider demons a species. I know it sounds romantic in theory, but we humans have been fighting about that very thing amongst ourselves forever.*

And how far have you gotten? she asked. *You still kill people over the color of their skin. I would have no chance.*

Well, I can't argue with you, but I would fight for you, Katie told her. *And throw your ashes somewhere pretty when you were evaporated.*

Right. She chuckled. *Like the city dump.*

It's on the list, Katie agreed.

You know what I need to do? Pandora sounded excited. *I need to start a bucket list, and on that list I will put having sex this high in the air.*

It's called the mile-high club. Katie snickered. *Many people have joined the mile-high club.*

I'm sure you haven't, prude. Pandora scoffed. *Though I have to say, I'm impressed there is already a name for it. You humans really are just simple carnal creatures.*

Right, but you understand that it's not just an opportunity to see how many different places you can have sex, right? Katie asked.

I mean, what else would it be? Pandora asked. *It's a sex bucket list. There are a whole lot of places on this planet I wanna get it on.*

Yeah, but who with? Katie asked.

Whoever! Pandora laughed. *Whoever I fancy at that moment.*

But there is so much more to sex than what you are trying to do, Katie disagreed.

Oh, no...not the romance thing again. Pandora sighed.

I'm serious, Katie continued. *It's about love. About being together in a way you aren't with most people. It's a connection, something that draws two people together, and a way for them to bond on a very intimate level. Love is amazing, and it makes sex that much better. I have had sex with someone I loved and someone I didn't, and the times with the person I loved were so much better. It was not only sensual, but it was freeing. I felt completely comfortable opening myself up to him. It's a feeling you can't put on a bucket list, that's for sure.*

Love? Pandora laughed. *Have you seen what demons are made of, Katie? Have you noticed any ingredients even remotely like love on the list?*

I think I have, Katie insisted. *I think when you aren't looking, you let the secret out every once in a while.*

Pandora chuckled. *Girl, whatever you are smoking, thank Ella for me.*

Stephanie and Joshua were standing on the sandy road in front of the old base. The sun was high in the sky. Suddenly a bunch of eighteen wheelers rolled over the hill, blowing their horns and heading right for the compound.

Behind them were hot rods, jacked-up cars, and motorcycles, everyone looking more than a bit out of place. Back at the old house Stephanie had made some connections with the gang members in the area.

She had gone straight over there when she found out what needed to happen, and offered cash money for anyone who would help with some "real labor."

The guys were more than happy to oblige, so they grabbed their friends and headed for the base. Stephanie stood in the center of the road holding a large stick in the air, wielding it like a conductor's baton. She was happy to have the company, happy to get the boys some cash, and really happy to get everything out of there before the military official was set to arrive. She knew it would be tight, but she wasn't going to give up.

Calvin stood to the side and watched as everyone parked and jumped out of—or off—their vehicles and gathered around Stephanie. She gave them all instructions about what had to happen, and sent them on their way to get the work done. She slapped the guys on the ass with her stick as they went past her, moving them in the right direction and putting a little pep in their step.

At first Calvin thought they were giving her hell, but after a while he realized they were playing around with her like she was with them. They all had an incredible amount of respect for the woman, and he figured it wasn't the first time that she had helped them out in one way or another.

The guys from the trucks operated the cranes, getting the heavy machines out of the building and into the beds of the semis.

The rest of the gang members and the ladies who were there to help were able to get most of the machinery out of the place and onto the trucks by midnight.

They hauled ass in and out of that building, impressing Calvin and making Stephanie very happy. When they were done, she handed each of them an envelope and gave them the address of where to drop the stuff.

While Stephanie took care of the guys Joshua slipped away, wandering back into the building and down the stairs.

The place was empty; no sign that he had even been there. The cabinet that had housed the weapons was gone, as was the equipment, and even his bed and desk. He felt sad, like he had been uprooted.

It had been the first time he had felt comfortable since his parents were alive. Stephanie came up to him and wrapped her arms around his shoulders from behind, resting her chin on them.

"Don't be sad," she told him. "This was just a building. This isn't your past, present, or future. All the girls, all the dreams, and everything else is on those trucks, barreling down the freeway and heading straight for your future." She stood back and walked around to face him. "I won't lie, this was a really great start. It was a way to get the business off the ground and give you a place to lay your head, but you were just in junior high here. Let's take you up a notch to high school, and when you get on your feet there, we'll boost you all the way to college."

"I suppose you're right," Joshua said reluctantly. "I think I feel good about the future. What happened here will always be in my head, but I am ready to start fresh. Move forward, you know?"

"Me too, darlin'," Stephanie responded. "And you did really good here."

"Oh, and speaking of the future…" Joshua began. "I am going to talk to Katie and the others, and I think they are going to be really excited. I was looking some stuff up the other day on the dark web, and I came across a site that sold guns and such. I almost didn't go to the site, but then I realized they might have what I need, and after about two hours of scrolling through their stuff I found these machines. They are made of a special super-strong and super-durable metal, and I think that they might be perfect machines to help create the 9mm bullets I promised Katie."

"That is fantastic," Stephanie exclaimed, putting her arm around his shoulder. "I think she will be very happy, and that is something we really need."

The two walked out of the building, shutting the lights off for the last time.

Korbin stood at the window watching the semis drive down the road. He had to give it to Stephanie; when she was given a task, she didn't give up until she accomplished it. He wasn't too sure of who she'd managed to hire, but she knew the importance of what they were doing so she had his trust.

He watched Joshua and Stephanie disappear back into the building, then went into the kitchen, grabbed a water, and headed back down to his office.

Once inside he plopped down in his chair and opened his drawers. Nothing remained that could incriminate him in any way. They knew what the place was for, but he had cleaned everything else out, including any paper trail. He clicked on his screen and waited for it to load, figuring he might as well clear out his email too. He probably had some emails to answer anyway, so he could kill two birds with one stone.

When the email had loaded he opened the first, a message from the higher-ups double-checking that everything was ready for the next day's visitors. Korbin sighed and wrote back, wishing they had a little more trust and faith in him. It was the part of the job he hated the most, smiling and placating the people with the checkbook. They were private citizens and he knew very little about them, but they ran the show and he had a job to do. He told them he had taken care of everything, being vague in his descriptions to keep the email safe just in case. He clicked Send and scrolled to the next, slightly nervous at seeing a familiar email address. It was his contact with the DEA; the agent who had covered his tracks not too long ago.

Korbin,

I hope this is finding you well. This came across my desk

early this morning and I wanted to know if they belong to you?
Find the videos attached.

Your friend at the DEA office

Korbin winced, rubbing his hands over his face before opening the attachments. There were three videos attached to the email and he slowly pulled each of them up, watching each from beginning to end. The first was of an active-shooter situation in a bank, which rolled into two very familiar faces walking inside.

Katie and Damian were saving the damn day.

The time stamp put it on the exact date they had been in LA, trying to be inconspicuous and hiding from the team leaders. The next video picked up just as Katie grabbed the butt of the gun and lifted the robber off his feet. Damian was in the foreground beating the hell out of another guy, then hitting him over the head with a metal pole.

The last video took the cake. It showed Katie throwing a knife into the last shooter's arm.

Korbin replayed the last video a second time and sighed, leaning back and shaking his head. He had told them to go and relax, not become the superheroes of LA while they were there.

When Damian had told him that they had helped the police with a bank robbery call he had assumed it was with tactics, not by disarming the assholes.

"Helping where they weren't supposed to," Korbin muttered.

As if he didn't have enough on his plate, he now had to worry about whether the videos had the potential to out Katie and Damian. Sure, the cops wouldn't know they were looking at demons, but their operation was black ops. It was under the radar, and they just might have shown themselves in the light.

Only a select group of people knew about them, which would make the videos very confusing to a judge who wasn't in the loop. They looked like crazed vigilantes who had rolled into a bank and saved the day by annihilating three criminals. No matter how many lives they had saved, they hadn't had his approval to do something like that.

Korbin sincerely wanted to kill them or rip them a new asshole, but they were already on their way to New York.

All he could hope was that the tapes got swept under the rug and they kept their noses clean while they were in the Big Apple. National incidents were not what the higher-ups needed to keep the whole thing going, nor would they appreciate "rogue" team members running around town saving everything that squealed.

Korbin pulled the email back up and began typing, letting the DEA agent know that the LAPD had requested they tell them when the team was in town in case they needed help.

He let her know he hadn't authorized it, and that he could not afford for his two best operatives to be implicated in the event. It needed to stay hush hush. He didn't know if it was something she could help him with, but he had to give it his best shot.

Then he skipped down a few lines and asked the most important question, not knowing if he really wanted the answer.

"Are these videos available to the public?"

14

Katie, Damian, and Ella looked out the window as the jet pulled into a private hangar; the same one Ella had been picked up from. They gathered their stuff, and Katie ignored Ella's loud sighs. She was just going to have to get used to it; there were no two ways about that. When they climbed out of the plane there was a tall guy wearing all black and leaning against the back of the SUV. He straightened as soon as the jet's door opened and walked toward them.

"Hi," he said, shaking all their hands. "I'm Isaac, the team second. John sent me to pick you guys up and bring you back to the base on the main island. Is there anything you guys need before we get there?"

"No, thanks." Katie smiled and elbowed Ella before she could speak.

"All right," he said, opening the back. "You can put your luggage in here, and we will get you set up back at base."

"Sounds good," Damian told him. "Thank you for taking us on such short notice."

"No problem at all," Isaac assured him. "Seems to be the name of the game in this business."

"Yeah." Damian shrugged.

"So how are you, Ella?" Isaac asked as he helped her into the SUV.

"Oh, just peachy. Just freaking *peachy*," she replied.

He chuckled. "I'm glad to see you still have your spark."

Once everyone had gotten into the vehicle, Isaac pulled out and made his way toward the City. Katie sat up front with him, watching as the buildings got taller and closer together. She had never been to New York besides the last fly-in, so it was exciting to see how it really looked. There were people and stores everywhere, and the taxis were just like the ones in the movies. They passed the entrance to Central Park and Katie smiled, watching the people rollerblading in the dry ice-skating rink. She had always wanted to go to New York in the winter time to see the lights, the trees, the snow, and the festivities. She watched all these movies at Christmas-time, and that was how she pictured Christmas in the rest of the world.

Growing up near Las Vegas was a drag when it came to winters. The coldest it normally got during the day was fifty, and it only reached freezing about one week out of every year. They got snow and you could watch it fall, but it always melted before it hit the ground. She had never seen a white Christmas in person, and the Santa in a t-shirt just wasn't the same as the warm red suit to her.

Even in the warm weather, though, New York was a

sight to see. Part of her wished that she would get the chance to stay there longer and really do some exploring.

She thought she would love walking around big cities and getting lost in the architecture, the sounds, and the amazing food. Well, the food part was Pandora, but would still make the experience that much better. She hoped she had a chance someday.

"So, you described the base like it wasn't the only one?" Katie asked.

Isaac smiled. "Yeah. We, uh…we actually have three bases in New York City alone. Or near it, at least. We have the one we are going to, which is here on the island, we have one on the other side over the bridge, and then we have one in New Jersey. Jersey City, to be exact."

"Why so many?" Katie asked. "Is this a serious stomping ground for demons?"

"Well, yeah, for smaller ones, and the covens here are fruitful for sure, but the traffic is the biggest problem," he explained. "It can take three hours to get through the tunnels sometimes. We had to spread out to be able to tackle the whole place. We have a larger team than most— twenty-one spots. It sounds like a lot to everyone, but I personally think it should be bigger than that. If you think about it, there are multiple fire departments in each area of the city, and they are full too. We should have just as many bases, but the higher-ups think that would cause too much noise."

"Right." Katie frowned. "I knew you guys covered a lot of territory, but I had no idea you had basically three teams in one."

Katie turned and looked back at Damian, wondering if

they should have gotten more weapons. He didn't read her mind like she had hoped, just stared back at her blankly.

"Why did this not come up in meetings?" Katie asked. "I didn't know that New York had the equivalent of three teams just in the City."

"Yeah," Damian admitted. "I mean, I knew that. I guess it just never came up." He shrugged. "I didn't even think about it."

"I suppose it's a good thing you have that many," Katie agreed, turning back around. "I mean, it would be nuts to take care of this city with just seven team members."

"Yeah." Isaac chuckled. "I don't think we would be able to do it with so few."

Just then his phone started to ring, and he excused himself and picked it up. Katie looked out the window, not wanting to be rude and eavesdrop. The buildings were so tall, and she wondered how they managed that when chasing demons. She immediately had more of an appreciation for their teams.

She felt overwhelmed at the compound and at the base; she didn't know how she would handle it in a city block like that. Even in LA things were spread farther apart. There were a million hiding places out there, and a million ways to find yourself in a really bad situation.

"We have to make a bit of a detour," Isaac told them. "There is a call for an exorcism not far from here, and since I have a priest I told them we would handle it. I hope that's all right, Damian."

"That's fine," Damian agreed. "We can give this little lady a taste of the big leagues."

"Oh, lord." Katie sighed. "She does not need to go on an exorcism yet."

"I was talking about *you*." Damian winked.

"Very funny," Katie replied.

"What?" Ella asked excitedly. "We are going on a call? I want to see this stuff go down."

"She hasn't been on a call yet?" Isaac asked.

"No," Katie admitted. "It's been slow back at home, and to be honest we are lucky to get her out of bed for training every day. I am not sure she is quite ready for a fight."

"I don't know if that is true," Ella said, "but I think I am definitely ready to be a spectator. How am I going to learn if I don't know what to expect? I mean, they just threw you in on your first incursion, Katie."

"Yeah, but I was dedicated to getting better," Katie answered. "I didn't try to escape out any windows. Besides, I remember my first exorcism; it was definitely not what I expected. In fact, I don't even know if I want to go to this thing. There were demons and souls, and a giant demon that had to be defeated. It was not like the movies. I would take Spinning Head Girl over what happened any day."

"That doesn't sound like a normal exorcism." Isaac laughed.

"Nothing *ever* seems to be normal for our team," Katie replied with a smile, turning back to Damian. "You remember the first 'date' you took me on?"

"Oh, lord." Damian laughed. "That was a doozy."

"What happened?" Ella asked.

"Well we got there for a run-of-the-mill exorcism of a house, and come to find out, the ghost hunters who tipped us off were infected," Katie explained. "The house was haunted or infected or something, and there was legit horror-movie craziness going on. The walls were bleeding, there was crazy laughter, and the doors would shut on their own. If that weren't enough, a giant demon came out, ready to kick our asses. We fought the damn thing for like hours and were eventually able to defeat it, but we pretty much demolished the house in the process. When we finally got back to the ghost hunters we were able to get the demons out and push them back to hell, but it was crazy. The ghost hunters were mad that they didn't get readings first."

"Assholes!" Ella exclaimed. "They should have been kissing your feet and thanking you for giving them their lives back. They could have been Damned, or even worse. This is why I hate people—seriously. They have no idea what it is like to be caught in a life like this—ungrateful jerks that they were. But that sounds nuts."

"It was." Katie laughed, winking at Damian. "It made me a better hunter, that's for sure. I had to use skills I didn't even know I possessed."

"I think that was one of the turning points for Katie," Damian agreed. "She blossomed there; showed she knew what she was up against. Trust me, though…she would not have gotten that one so good if she hadn't been training so hard. This girl was training night and day: down there working with weapons, running, hitting the weights, and learning new moves. She knew her life was on the line, so she threw herself into it."

"I didn't like working out. Not many people do, but I wanted to survive, and I knew that being at my physical peak was incredibly important, so I kicked my own ass." Katie smiled.

"Well, maybe it isn't as bad as it seems," Ella said, watching out the window. "Maybe I'll think differently after this."

Korbin paced his office floor, thinking of all the things that he should remember while the military was there. He knew he shouldn't be nervous. They weren't his bosses, but he understood that if they were pissed off they could give him a really hard time, and he really didn't want that kind of drama on his hands.

He had been so close to being out of there, but they had gotten to him first. They would have a ton of questions, and he knew what he had to answer and what he could keep hidden, but he still didn't like the intrusion—especially when he had so many other things going on.

Just then his phone buzzed in his pocket and he pulled it out, looking at the notification of incoming email. It was from the agent and he was almost afraid to open it, but he did. He sat down and sighed before he read it, hoping like hell for good news.

Apparently the videos from the bank were *not* out in public, at least not that they had found while searching. The tapes had been confiscated after the crime, and immediately put into evidence.

Korbin blew out a breath in relief, then leaned his head back, closed his eyes, and mouthed the words "Thank you" to the heavens.

It was about time they had some sort of good luck, even if it was in a situation they should have never gotten themselves into in the first place. He was definitely going to have a talk with those two when everything had settled down.

He didn't need his two vigilantes running all over the country solving crimes for the cops. They were demon hunters, and that day they should only have helped if it was demon-related *and* absolutely necessary. They had made enough waves in LA already; they didn't need to start anymore.

He opened his eyes and continued reading the email.

The video was taken to the Los Angeles Police Department, she wrote.

It was stashed in the need-to-know section, and I happened upon it. The department really appreciated the help, since there were many souls in that bank and that situation could have been a hell of a lot worse than it was. No one was killed, and the officer who was shot is expected to make a full recovery. Neither the department nor the DEA will let the tapes leak, but somehow they need to figure out how to keep things like this under wraps. If this situation occurs again, we want to be able to keep it out of the public eye. Sometimes these things can move quickly, and videos can pop up before they even get back to the station.

There did need to be some sort of process for keeping these things out of the public eye, but at what cost?

The real solution to the problem was keeping the D Squad out of incidents that didn't have anything to do with demons. Korbin didn't wish harm to any of the people in the bank, that was for sure, and he was proud of both Katie and Damian for taking the initiative to help in a situation that was obviously dire, but they had to think about *their* cause, too.

The demons threatened the very existence of the human race, and that made it very important for the team to stay out of things that could expose them. He didn't know how to tell them to leave a bank full of people to possibly die, but they needed to practice discretion.

As it was, it looked like the department was hoping they would be around again if something like that occurred. They were treading in dangerous territory with that, making it look like they could rely on the team to help in any old case they couldn't handle. The reality of it was that most things needed to be handled by someone else, though.

"We aren't frickin' superheroes, after all," Korbin muttered, putting his phone back in his pocket.

He got up from his chair and walked back up to the main area, staring out the window into the desert. The lights inside the house were off, and the moon was full in the sky.

It was a beautiful night; there was a lunar blue glow that kind of cascaded over the hilly desert. He was going to miss this place. He had put blood, sweat, and tears into making it a home, and in one fell swoop it had been almost completely demolished.

The new place was going to be good—good for the team and good for the country—but that didn't mean he wouldn't feel homesick for a while. The new base would eventually become comfortable, but until then he had to protect their secrets—and that was exactly what he was about to face.

15

Isaac pulled up to the curb and parked the SUV like a pro.

Katie knew she couldn't drive in a place like New York. She could barely parallel park her car at the compound.

She looked out the window at the tall brownstone that was their destination. The windows were dark, and the atmosphere eerie. She really hoped it didn't go the way that it had in the past because, she wasn't in the mood for a fight.

The four of them got out of the car. Katie had her knives, and she was fine with those. Damian had his bible and his cross, and Isaac had what he wanted. Ella didn't need a weapon, because Katie would make sure she got her out of there if things got hairy.

When they got up to the door, Isaac looked back at them and nodded. He opened it and they crept into the house as the lights inside began to flicker.

The demon already knew they were there, but they had to find the host before it found them. A sound from up the stairs to the right caught Damian's attention, and he motioned for the others to follow behind him.

When they reached the second floor, they followed the groaning and screaming to a bedroom at the end of the hall on the righthand side. Inside was a woman somewhere in her forties, who had long red hair and was dressed in a long white nightgown.

The room was almost empty, not what Katie had expected from the expensive brownstone in that part of town. There was a bed and a night stand, but nothing else except a cross hanging lopsided on the adjacent wall.

The woman growled and groaned, her body twitching and writhing on the bed.

She looked as if she were in pain, which was not what Katie had expected at all. The four slowly moved closer, Damian providing instruction.

He walked over and pushed her head down on the bed, then pulled her eyelids back to reveal nothing but white. He turned to the other three and nodded.

"Katie, I want you to assist. Isaac, stand back with Ella. Watch, but don't interfere unless I ask. If things get bad, take Ella and get out. Katie and I can handle it."

"Got it," Isaac agreed, pulling Ella over to the corner. He kept his hand on his weapon.

"Katie," Damian turned to her, "I want you to hold her down and keep her down until I can latch onto this demon. I might need Pandora's help."

"Okay." Katie nodded, feeling nervous for the first time in a while.

Don't be nervous, Pandora told her. *You've faced worse.*

Easier said than done, Katie replied.

Katie walked over to the bed and looked at the woman, then pushed her shoulders down firmly, pressing her top half to the bed despite her writhing. Damian nodded and walked around the bed, pulling out his cross and opening his bible.

"*Oratio ad Sancte Michaelem Archangelum in nomine Patris, et Filii, et Spiritu sancto. Amen,*" Damian chanted in Latin.

The woman strained against Katie's hands and foam spewed from her mouth.

Katie gasped when her eyes shot open and there was a bright-red circle around her pupils. She looked straight up at Katie, and she could feel the stare burning into her soul. She closed her eyes for a moment, but when she opened them again the woman was still glaring up at her.

"*Princeps gloriosissime caelestis exercitus, Sancte Michaelem Archangelum, da nobis aciem adversus principes potestates principes autem adversus mundi rectores tenebrarum harum, contra spiritualia nequitiae, in caelestibus,*" Damian continued.

The woman screamed and her body went stiff, her eyes shining brightly in the dimly-lit room. She breathed heavily, looking at Katie with a malicious grin moving across her broken and chapped lips.

Katie began to sweat, her hands slipping down the woman's shoulders to reveal deep lacerations to her skin, maybe a week old.

"Fuck you," the demon growled. "I've heard about you two. Fuck you, Katie. Fuck you, Pandora, if that's what you're calling yourself now."

Katie hissed, trying to hold it together as gray liquid oozed from the woman's mouth and she laughed deeply in a voice not her own.

Take a deep breath, Pandora said. *You are okay. This bastard is going to get what he has coming to him. I'm taking over.*

No, Katie replied. *Not in front of Isaac.*

"*Nos eiciam vos de nobis, quicumque haec legis, Et spiritus immundi, omnis satanica potestates. Omnes infernales impletis, improbis legionibus necnon sectarum numerum pervenitur.*" Damian raised his hands and screamed, "We drive you from us, whoever you may be, unclean spirits, all satanic powers, all infernal invaders, all wicked legions, assemblies, and sects!"

At that moment the room began to shake around them as if it weren't attached to the rest of the house. Damian pulled out his cross and held it in the air as he pressed his hand to the woman's chest.

The woman spat and screamed.

Katie watched as the demon rose from her body, shrieking and scowling, its eyes as red as blood. Katie had never seen anything like it, and she never wanted to again. The demon howled as its spirit was sucked back down into hell, finally disappearing.

The woman laid still and Katie let go, backing up against the wall and shaking her head. It had terrified her in a way she didn't understand.

It's okay, Pandora whispered. *Some of us are way more tortured than others. Take a deep breath.*

Katie nodded and glanced at Ella, remembering that the girl was watching. Katie pulled her shirt straight and closed her eyes, swallowing hard and pushing away the tears that wanted to spring forth.

She looked at Damian, who nodded and smiled before sitting down on the edge of the bed to check on the woman. She was still alive, and from the looks of her pink cheeks she was going to be just fine.

"She will recover," Damian whispered. "That was a scary one, I know."

"He was so *angry*," Katie whispered.

"Some of them are. I could tell this one had a very tortured soul. You did well, thank you."

Katie nodded, having gained a whole new respect for Damian. This trip was definitely turning out a lot different than she had thought.

She had expected to come to New York, maybe kill a couple of demons, train Ella a bit more, and then head back home. She hadn't expected to witness something like what had just taken place. She wasn't quite sure why it bothered her so much. She had seen demons eat people, after all, but this was different. This woman had reminded her of her mother, trying to fight off something that was stronger than her.

Pandora had been kind—talking her down during the whole thing—but part of her wondered if Pandora was capable of taking over someone's body like that, forcing them to do and say horrible things.

She shook the thought from her head and walked over to Isaac and Ella. Isaac smiled at Katie and patted her on the shoulder, having seen the horror she had witnessed up close.

She turned to Ella, expecting her to be terrified, but instead she looked absolutely enthralled.

"That was fucking amazing!" Ella exclaimed. "Like, he just grabbed that demon out of her chest and *bam!*" She clapped her hands together. "It was *gone*. And the woman is going to be okay, which blows my damn mind."

Ella had never seen something like that before, at least not in real life, and until that moment had not thought it might be real.

She had heard rumors of exorcisms, but she thought it was complete bullshit just like everything else that went along with religion; fairytales meant to scare children into their beds at night.

She could tell that everyone was afraid it was going to scare her off, but it did the opposite. It made her want to *fight*, to kick demon ass just like the rest of them did. It made her want to buckle down and get going, because there was no time to waste.

Did you see that? Ella asked Melneck. *That was* crazy!

Yes, yes. He yawned. *To be honest, I found the whole thing quite boring. It looked like a poor remake of Amityville Horror. I've seen seventeenth-century plays with better sound effects and props.*

Oh, stop showing off, she replied.

Oh, you haven't seen anything yet, sweetheart. He chuckled. *You have no idea what I can do.*

"She will need watching." Damian was talking to the New York team member. "At least until she comes to—just to make sure that the demon didn't do any real damage to her body. Those cuts look about a week old, so she must have been lurking around here possessed all this time."

Isaac nodded. "No problem. I'll call it in, and they will send someone over here to keep an eye on her."

"Thank you." Damian patted him on the shoulder.

Katie stood in the corner with Ella, not saying much as Damian covered the woman with blankets and wiped the drool and vomit off her. He bent to her side and said a prayer before Isaac walked back in holding his phone. Damian rose and looked at him.

"He will be here in ten minutes," Isaac told the priest.

"Good, we can wait around that long," he replied. "Then let's go get some food."

"Perfect," Isaac agreed.

Katie was entranced watching the woman sleep, lying perfectly still in her bedroom. She had been a different person just minutes before, all because of that demon. It was still plaguing her, and she didn't know why.

"Katie," Ella called from the door a few minutes later. "You coming?"

"Yeah," Katie said, shaking the thoughts and following her down to the SUV.

They all piled inside and headed over to a bar Damian knew. It wasn't very crowded, or at least not as crowded as Katie thought it would be in a city like that. When they walked in, she realized that it seemed to be a hangout for people like them. Isaac smiled and waved at a few customers, and the four of them took a seat in a back table.

"This is one of my favorite bars," Damian offered. "I have a favorite bar in twenty-one different cities."

"A priest who drinks?" Ella whispered, leaning toward Katie but keeping her eyes on Damian.

"Apparently a lot of them do," she whispered back.

The waitress brought menus out and handed them around. Ella looked up and down the menu, her mouth watering for some cheese fries and nachos. Melneck put a stop to that, though.

This food is disgusting. He sniffed. *Made with canned things and weird packaged meats.*

Ella laughed. *It's bar food.*

Yes, well, that's where it will stay, he replied. *You need to focus on putting into your mouth the best and most wholesome food you can.*

I am going to put cheese fries in it right now, Ella argued.

No, you are going to put a salad in it, no cheese, light vinaigrette dressing, Melneck replied.

Uh...hell, no, she snarled.

Don't make me step on your intestines again, he threatened.

Fine, she growled, *but I get to keep the cheese, and I get ranch dressing.*

Light Ranch, he compromised. *And the only reason I am giving in is because I don't want you to make a scene.*

Fine, Ella snapped, *but you are a dick.*

Katie sat quietly in the corner across the table, seeing that Ella was talking to her demon. She smiled, remembering when Derek had told her she had looked like she was talking to herself at the sex shop in Vegas. It felt like a million years ago.

Thank you for back there, Katie told Pandora.

Don't mention it, she replied. *So, what are we going to eat?*

I was thinking a cheeseburger and cheese fries.

Whaaat? Pandora gasped. *You want what I want? I am rubbing off on you.*

You are literally inside me, Katie replied. *There can't be that much rubbing going on.*

Pandora laughed. *True.*

So, have you ever been to New York City before? Katie asked.

Actually I have, Pandora replied. *It was a long time ago, though—maybe 1844 or 1845. It looked much different then. I was dating this lovely guy; strange, but lovely. His name was Edgar. He had a brownstone over on 3rd Street. If I remember right, it was 85 West 3rd.*

Katie laughed. *You have a good memory.*

Yeah, well, Edgar was too much fun to forget. She chuckled. *We would drink and laugh, and drink more, and have sex, and then laugh more. He was the closest thing to a friend I'd had in a long time at that point. We met in the city at a party. He hated parties; liked to be alone in his room. He was one of those starving artist types. I think he was a writer. Yes, a writer. We had a lot of fun together, seeing the sights during the day and just sitting around talking all night long. I swear he never slept, except for when he would pass out after all the wine I would feed him. He always tried to keep up with me, the silly thing, not realizing I metabolized alcohol much differently than he did.*

It sounds like you really liked him.

As much as a demon can like a human, I suppose, she said.

He definitely liked me. Wrote some stories with me in them. At the time, though, no one really cared who he was. He had big eyes and dark hair, and never really came out of that brownstone. I guess he was the epitome of becoming famous after death.

Why do you say that? Katie asked.

I remember seeing one of his stories last time I was up here, she said. *It was in the seventies, and I wandered into a bookstore and saw his picture on the wall. I asked the clerk, and she looked shocked that I didn't know he was famous. She pulled out what was apparently his most famous work—The Raven, or something like that. Turns out he was very well known.*

Wait… Katie tried to keep a straight face. *You were dating* Edgar Allen Poe?

Mmmhmm, Pandora agreed as the waitress came back with the food.

That is insane, Katie replied.

It was fun, she said. *Oooh, look...they put bacon on the fries!*

Just which Seventies was Pandora talking about?

16

Korbin stood next to Calvin on the roof of the building looking over the scene. There was still some debris, but they had managed to clean it up pretty well since the whole event happened.

Calvin was motionless, obviously nervous about what was going on, but Korbin had managed to calm himself before the sun came up. He knew he was in a position where he didn't have to really explain himself, but he would be as hospitable as possible.

"There they are," Calvin said, looking off in the distance.

Over the horizon from the north came three military helicopters choppering in. It looked like a scene from a movie, sand blowing around as they landed in the clearing below them. The pilots switched off the engines and Korbin turned to Calvin with a strained smile on his face.

"You ready to go greet our guests?" he asked through clenched teeth.

"Never been *less* ready to do something," Calvin answered.

"We'll be fine." Korbin laughed, slapped him on the shoulder, and turned for the door. "Come on, let's get this over with, I'm tired of all the suspense."

They headed down through the building and out the front doors to greet the guests exiting the helicopters.

First was a woman dressed in Army Blues with a colonel's insignia on the shoulders. She had ribbons pinned in rows on the front of her coat, and her beret was slightly tipped to the side. Behind her was a general wearing Blues as well, with even more ribbons and stars on the shoulders of his jacket. He was an older man with white hair and a weathered face, while she was younger, her dark hair pulled back perfectly at the nape of her neck.

"Korbin," the general said. "I'm General Aaron Brushwood, and this is Colonel Karen Jehovivich. It's good to finally meet you."

"You as well," he said, shaking their hands. "And this is my Team Lead Two, Calvin Turnbuckle."

"Nice to meet you," the general replied, shaking Calvin's hand.

The general and colonel were not only new to the teams, but new to their positions. Korbin led the two inside the building, where it was a lot less noisy. The general took off his cover and placed it under his arm, looking around the entry.

"I am aware that in the past, relationships between the military teams and your own have been strained, to say the least," the general admitted. "I hope that can change between us."

"As do I," Korbin replied carefully. "I *do* have to ask why you decided to come here now."

"Well, I heard through the grapevine that there had been a major incursion here, and I would like to understand what happened," he explained. "The more knowledge I have on what your teams do, the better we can all work together."

"Okay," Korbin replied. "And what are you looking to learn, exactly?"

"Well, first, why *you* were targeted out of everyone, including the military teams. It just seemed strange that your base would have been the bullseye," he said. "I'm interested to know what you did about it, and I'd like to know if we are sure that none of them got away?"

Korbin just stood there a moment, trying to parse what the general was asking. It almost sounded like he was questioning Korbin's competency in his own house. He didn't appreciate being questioned. He had put his life on the line for their country both before and since he had joined the teams.

He had seen more combat than most soldiers would see in their entire careers, and he had more than proved himself to be a competent leader.

Calvin cleared his throat, feeling the tension.

"General, with all due respect, you question me as if I were a student." Korbin's eyes narrowed. "I sent the military the necessary documents, including the after-action report that we all agreed five years ago would be part of us operating a private mercenary squad to fight the demons. There was more than enough information in those documents to answer any and all questions without you having to fly out here like this. I am, as it were, *not* under your command."

"Very true, Korbin," the general agreed, playing nice. "You are not under my command; you are a private citizen. However, I am standing on US soil, and there are foreigners—aliens if you will—who are attacking people on my watch. Can you understand why I would want to see the place for myself? And questions may arise. I am not the firing squad. I am just here to get to the bottom of things."

"There is nothing more to tell you beyond what was in that statement, sir," Korbin replied. "This is actually *not* US government land. It is private land, bought and paid for by myself and our higher-ups; also documented with the government. We have gone through this time and time again, which was why we had the Senate hearing just five years ago—to determine the rules and regulations under which the teams operate."

"Well," the general looked down at his cover, "it seems we are at an impasse, then."

"It seems that way," Korbin agreed, standing tall.

"May I take a look at the damaged buildings to the right of this one?" the colonel asked, interrupting the awkward silence.

The three men looked through the open door at the buildings Katie and the big demon had destroyed during their battle to the death. The colonel apparently had a good eye for detail, and though the area had been largely picked up, Korbin didn't want to show her. He knew it was clear of all evidence, though.

Regardless, she had guessed what had likely caused the

damage—which ultimately made her more dangerous than the general.

"I am assuming they were knocked down by one of the…" she paused and opened a folder, "three large demons who escaped the portal."

"They were," Korbin confirmed, glancing at Calvin. "It happened during a fight at the end of the battle. My team managed to take the beast down, but not without infrastructure destruction."

"Right," she agreed. "But how did the buildings get so *damaged*? It would take brute force to knock those down. They are stone and cinderblock construction."

"To be honest, Colonel," Calvin interjected. "Neither Korbin nor myself were part of that battle, so we can't give eyewitness accounts. Those are in the file, and anything we added would be mere speculation."

"So, who *was* in that part of the fight?" she asked.

"That would be Katie, Jeremy, and Eric," Korbin replied. "Only Eric is here right now. Katie is taking care of business elsewhere, and Jeremy is deceased."

She grimaced. "I'm sorry. However, I would like to speak to Eric later."

"Of course," Korbin replied. "Why don't I give you a tour of the main area, and then we can move on to the unstable areas."

The general and the colonel both nodded, so Korbin and Calvin led them up to the main living quarters first. As Korbin talked about the battle and what had happened there, Calvin slipped off down the hall and snuck quietly into Eric's room. Eric looked up at him in confusion, and

Calvin put his finger over his lips. He inched forward and leaned down.

"I think you should disappear for a little while," he whispered, "to avoid any conflict or unnecessary questioning. When we go down to the pit, take the SUV and head into town for a bit. I'll call you when the coast is clear."

"All righty," he agreed, and Calvin slipped back out the door.

Calvin caught back up with them before they even noticed he was gone, and they headed down to the training area to continue the tour.

When they were done with that, they went back up to the living quarters to allow the colonel to speak with Eric. Calvin led her to his room and knocked on the door, but there was no reply. Slowly he opened it, and blessed Eric in his head when the room was empty.

"That's strange," Calvin remarked. "He must have gone out."

"What's that?" Korbin asked as he walked up.

"Eric isn't here," Calvin told him.

"That's strange," Korbin repeated, surprised. "I asked him to stick around. He must have had an important call or something take him away. Hopefully he will be back before you leave."

It was obvious that they were suspicious, but they kept their thoughts to themselves. Korbin was either a damned good liar, which was possible, or he really didn't know that the man had left.

The four of them headed to the ruined buildings and did a tour and checked one more time to see if Eric had returned before walking the general and colonel back out to the helicopters. Calvin and Korbin stood quietly until the choppers were speeding off, then Korbin dropped his hands and growled angrily.

"How did they know all that?" Calvin asked.

"I'll tell you how," Korbin snarled. "Either they have bugs here in our base, or someone I spoke to from the other teams updated the military. Either way you look at it, there are spies in the ranks of the Damned."

Katie breathed in the smell of the city. She was enjoying a stroll through the streets: listening to the cars honking, smelling the mixture of car exhaust and hot dog stands, and just being a tourist for a moment. Pandora was excited to be back, but was absolutely shocked at how different everything was from the last time she had been there.

Katie still couldn't believe that she had dated Edgar Allen Poe.

You know what I don't understand? Pandora asked. *Why there is a damn Dunkin' Donuts on nearly every corner?*

People like their donuts, I guess. Katie laughed.

It's like someone decided that those were the only donuts we were allowed to eat, and then they built one on every corner to make it impossible for the competition, she griped.

Yeah, Katie replied. *Welcome to the American way. Besides, you are just upset because you really don't like Dunkin Donuts. If it were any other donut shop, you would be all about it. You would be in heaven, and I probably would have to talk you out of moving here.*

You are damn right I don't like them, Pandora snapped.

Sure, it's round and it has a hole in it and it's made of dough, but these are not high-quality donuts. They are not made by hand every morning. I read that the dough is shipped to them, and they just put it in the proofer and oven. While they are being lazy, there are hardworking donut-makers out there mixing and preparing every morning.

You are really passionate about this. Katie laughed. *I mean, it's just a donut. I think I created a monster. Or worse, I created a donut snob.* Katie thought for a moment. *You are a damned donut snob, which I didn't even think could be a thing.*

I don't know what the hell you are talking about, Pandora retorted. *I am all kinds of snob. Donut snob, sex snob, length-and-girth snob, Italian food snob, and the list goes on. I mean, I could seriously be a snob about underwear, hair, makeup, jelly, jam—which I still don't know the difference between—toast, cars, and just about anything else, really.*

You seriously need to relax and just enjoy things. Katie laughed and bought another piece of pizza. *For example, we are walking around tasting all the different slices. I am not a snob because the last place sucked; they just have sucky pizza— that's on them. You can't change these things, so why get so uptight and upset about it? I just move on to the next slice, and if it's that bad, I toss it. Plain and simple.*

That is the exact definition of you. Pandora scoffed. *"Plain and freaking simple." If you don't have standards for your pizza and for your donuts, what do you stand for?*

You know, there was a place I ate at when I was a kid that took pizza dough, rolled it into balls, deep fried it, and served it as donut holes, Katie told her.

That is disgusting, and frankly, I am offended, Pandora shot back. *Who were those people? I do have to admit though, I am more than enjoying our exploration of New York pizza. And don't worry, it's not going to your ass.*

Please stay away from my boobs too, at least for now, Katie whined. Like seriously...these things are getting heavy. They look great, but I'm gonna have back problems.

Fine, the demon said, exasperated. *I swear, you are the hardest person to please. I give you curves, a flat stomach, a perfect ass, and tits a plastic surgeon can't replicate, and you still complain.*

Katie laughed and kept walking. She was looking ahead at a kid standing next to his mom, playing on his tablet, when suddenly a man in rough clothes with a long scraggly beard lunged forward and grabbed the tablet right out of the kid's hand. The mom yelled, but no one else made any kind of move to help.

Katie popped the rest of the pizza in her mouth and wiped off her hands as the guy ran toward her.

When he got close enough she calmly reached out and grabbed him by the throat with one hand, using the other to punch him three times in the face. Before she let him go, she grabbed the tablet from his hands.

"I'll take that, thank you." She dropped him to the sidewalk, where he lay unconscious.

She nonchalantly walked up to the kid and handed him the tablet, then patted him on the head and continued past him like it had been no big deal.

Pandora giggled.

Everyone stopped what they were doing and stared at her as she walked away, having no clue what to do or what had just happened.

Finally a cop ran up, trying to figure out why the man

was on the sidewalk. The mother told him what had happened, and everyone pointed in Katie's direction. For a moment Katie was nervous, but the cop looking down at the perp, shrugged, and nodded.

Apparently he thought the man had gotten exactly what was coming to him. Katie was just glad she could help.

You could be a vigilante in this town. A real superhero, even, Pandora suggested. *You could wear a mask and call yourself "Donut Girl."*

Nope, nope, nope. Katie laughed, tossed her napkin in the trash, and walked around the corner.

17

"Melvin," Ella squealed happily as he entered the training center. "It's been a while now. Go on anymore hot demon dates?"

One of the guys off to the side snickered.

"Great, now *you* are making fun of me too," he growled, walking up to Damian and sticking his hand out. "How are you doing, Damian? Long time no see."

"Haven't been out this way in some time." He smiled as he returned the handshake. "Good to see you, and thank you for saving this one's fragile ass."

"Hey, I'm not fragile! I just need some work, that's all," Ella grumped.

"That's a bit of a change of heart." Melvin chuckled. "Las Vegas push your mind into the right place?"

"Nah, that happened last night when I got to see an exorcism," she told him, moving her arms around like a stupid version of Frankenstein's monster. "The demon was all crazy, teeth bared, snarling, and cursing everyone in the room. It was awesome."

"All right then." Melvin laughed. "I don't know if I would describe an exorcism as 'awesome' but whatever gets you motivated, I suppose." He turned his attention to Damian. "Did the infected live?"

"Yeah," Damian answered, leading them onto the floor. "She is a bit the worse for wear, but one of your guys watched her till she woke up and got her bandaged. Told her she had gotten hit by something, and he brought her home. She was a little confused, but she ended up settling down."

"Good, then I call it a success," Melvin remarked, turning to Ella. "Now, what are we going to do with you? I see you've acquired some workout clothes…"

He looked down at her shoes.

"Although you apparently don't like tennis shoes," he finished as she wiggled her toes in her boots. "No matter, we can work with that."

The guys in the gym took her to the side to show her some basic protective moves, feeling it was most important to understand how to protect herself. Melneck monitored her movements, giving her pointers here and there on how to turn her body, position her hands, and move her feet. It looked to Damian and Melvin like she was doing well, but she was having trouble with Melneck's instructions.

If you would just fucking slow down, I would be able to understand you, Ella griped.

Slow down? He scoffed. *Do you think the demons are going to slow down when you are fighting them?*

I know they won't, but could I at least learn the technique before you start hounding me? she grumbled. *There are no demons here to fight right this second.*

I personally think this is a waste of time. He sniffed. *I would start you off in some Tai Kwon Do, get the muscle memory down.*

That discipline is just for show, Ella argued. *I need something like Jiu Jitsu for fighting. I don't need useless techniques.*

First of all, Tai Kwon Do is not *useless. It's the most-used martial arts style in your puny little world,* Melneck informed her. *And secondly, Jiu Jitsu will do you no good unless you can get those demons on the ground. Sure, the small ones you can, but what about the big ones? You'll never get them on their backs. You could probably use the rolling techniques for faster movements, but the rest will be a waste, and might even get you killed.*

Then what do you want me to do? Ella asked. *Because boxing isn't going to work. I need a real combat technique— something that is down and dirty—because these guys, they don't play by the rules. If I do, I'll get myself killed. I mean, I'm small and lean, and I can move pretty fast.*

All right, all right, Melneck said, thinking. *I know! I should have thought of this first. Krav Maga will be your best friend.*

Sounds like a food. Ella snickered.

Far from it, though you might not like the training. It was created by the Israeli Defense Force for close combat. It's down and dirty, all right. Kicks in the nuts and, pokes in the eyes. The training pushes you to your limits and then past them.

Well, I'm probably going to be tired for the rest of my life anyway, Ella bitched. *I might as well be tired and able to kick the shit out of someone.*

"So, I think I know what kind of fighting I want to learn," Ella told Melvin.

"All right, whatcha got?" he asked.

"Krav Maga. It is combat-oriented, will push me to my limits, and best of all, it will make me a badass fighter."

"Hmm…" Melvin walked around her. "I like that idea, though I don't know if you can handle it."

"I got this," Ella assured him confidently.

"All right." He shrugged, keeping the smirk off his lips. "We'll train you, but I need to get my teammate Cody in on this, since he is the martial arts specialist. Some of the other team members in the New York area can come help train too. I like your motivation. Keep it up!"

Ella smiled at Damian and he winked, proud that she had started to come around.

As Stephanie sped through the desert, there was nothing on either side of them but sand and sun. They were headed to the new property, and Joshua was excited but also nervous to see his new home.

Joshua glanced back at Avery, one of Stephanie's girls, who was sitting in the back of the car. He was taking the forced time off as a good thing, just relaxing and helping wherever he could. Stephanie turned left through some broken-down gates and headed down a long-paved road. Ahead in the distance were the buildings, painted to blend with the sand. They were of a plain style, but large.

"This was an old ICBM base back in the day," Stephanie explained.

"What is 'ICBM?'" Avery asked.

"Intercontinental ballistic missile," Joshua answered. "They were big weapons, or rather *are* big weapons, and we built bases specifically to assemble, test, fire, and control them. This looks like it was one of the older ones."

"It was," Stephanie said. "Older, I mean, but at the same time it is pretty badass. I bought it after they decommissioned it years ago. I guess when you come from a cult like I did, you always assume that the future will be bleak. I wanted a place I could come to and be safe from everyone and everything. In my mind, there was nothing safer than a military installation that provided security for a weapon like that. This one was completely off-grid. The government never let anyone know it was out here."

They pulled up in front of one of the big buildings in the center and got out of the car, looking around them.

All of the remaining buildings were in reasonable shape on the outside and there hadn't been a ton of trash left behind. There was more than enough space to build whatever they wanted. Stephanie stared up at the bright blue sky, closing her eyes and enjoying the sun for a moment.

"I spent some time here cleaning it up a few years ago, and every three months I come back to make sure it's still in working condition." Stephanie looked at Joshua and Avery. "We will need to do more with it. I can tell you that it has functioning generators and water systems that provide power, heating, and cooling; the basics. I suggest we figure out if Amazon delivers here for the rest of it."

"What about the machines?" Joshua asked.

"Well," Stephanie said, pointing into the distance, "over that way there are some pretty good cement slabs from the buildings they took with them when they left. I think it would be a good area to place the machines on their pallets until we lay the foundation for the manufacturing building.

That's supposed to happen in three days, with a seven-day drying time. We can't put anything at the new place until the cement has cured."

"Okay…" Joshua looked up at the sky, thinking about the weather.

"I can tell you are worrying about them." She smiled. "Maybe we can get some supersized tents to cover them."

"It should only take a week or a week and a half for the power company to come out and run some of the grid that we need," Joshua said.

"The power comes within three miles of here, I think, since the old cables aren't efficient anymore." Stephanie peered into the distance. "It is going to cost a pretty penny to get them to run it the rest of the way. I never needed it, since I assumed power wouldn't be available when I really needed to come here. I was planning for a doomsday scenario, not a vacation home—or a place to house a demon-killing team."

She laughed, thinking about how much her life had changed.

Just months before she had been sending in clients for Avery to "take care of," and now she was overseeing a huge paramilitary installation. She was glad, though, to have put that part of her life behind her.

There was no longer anything in that world for her, and now that she had a better sense of self and better control over her abilities, she didn't feel like she needed to have a secret hideaway anymore.

She was more than happy to give it to her team.

"So, what does Korbin think about this bill?" Joshua asked. "I know he isn't a big fan of massive spending."

Stephanie smirked. "Who said we told him what the bill was going to be?"

———

"This team is pretty extensive," John said, looking at Damian and Katie. "There is a lot going on here the higher-ups don't really understand. Sometimes we have to work with the military, sometimes we are too late, and sometimes we don't get the call at all. It can be a hassle."

"I can't even imagine running one team, much less three, in an area like this," Katie admitted.

"It definitely gets busy." John chuckled. "We rarely go three nights without a call. There was only that exorcism last night, which was a very light night. Usually we would be racing from that call right over to another one, but luckily it didn't happen that way. They told me how well you guys did with that call, by the way. I appreciate you taking it. I know it had to be a pain getting off a plane and rolling right into something like that."

"It's all part of the job," Damian assured him. "I have to say, though, you have some pretty angry demons here."

"Yeah." John nodded. "They get really rowdy."

"So, what's next?" Katie asked. "You have us for a few days to help wherever we can."

"I was actually going to ask if you wouldn't mind going to the New Jersey side." John raised an eyebrow. "I am pretty low over there right now team-wise, and we have missed some pretty big calls. There might be some false alarms, but it's better to check them out than let them go and end up with a demon running loose."

"Absolutely," Damian told him. "And sure. We are up for that, right, Katie?"

Katie nodded. "Definitely."

"Would you take Ella with you?" John asked. "Let her get a real-world feeling for everything. I know she saw the exorcism yesterday, but I don't think that's a good representation of what we normally do. It was more like an introduction than anything else."

"Absolutely," Katie replied. "I think the girl needs some serious training, and taking her out with us might give that to her. I can go over the signs and what to look for, and keep her as safe as possible if we have to do any fighting."

"Perfect," John said, standing up from his desk. "Take any of the SUVs you want. There is GPS, just like at home. Call in when you get to Jersey City and we will go from there."

"Great." Katie stood up and shook his hand.

Katie and Damian grabbed Ella, who was standing near the office waiting for them to come back out, and headed to the garage.

They hopped into the SUV and programmed the GPS to get them to Jersey City from downtown Manhattan. It took them a bit to get a handle on things, since New York traffic was a bit different than anywhere else.

Damian squeezed the steering wheel tightly as they entered the tunnel and cruised toward the bridge.

When they finally made it to the Jersey base the place was bustling, but there were only five men instead of seven. They introduced themselves and were directed to the intake rooms, where they were handed vests and shown the way to the armory. When they were ready they sat down in a large glass room, waiting to be shown back up to the main area.

"You know, I've never been a redshirt before." Damian chuckled.

"Me either," Katie said.

"Why did they call us 'the redshirts' anyway?" Ella asked.

"Well, on Star Trek the redshirts were the people who were probably going to die," Damian explained with a smirk. "It's a morbid-sense-of-humor type of thing. We do that from time to time to keep our sanity. It's not like we believe it jinxes you—or at least I don't think so. There are people who refuse to be on redshirt teams; they won't take the assignment because they are superstitious in that way. I personally never have because the priest is usually the last to be picked for something like that. It is usually the standbys or the extra members who end up as redshirts, and since I don't leave Vegas much unless I'm on official business, I don't get called on for things like this. In reality, the shirts simply distinguish us from the others, since our faces are unknown and they don't want any friendly-fire situations. But like I said, it's not a jinx, just a joke."

"Except for those two in Los Angeles," Katie reminded him.

"You weren't supposed to mention that." Damian rolled his eyes and smacked Katie.

"Oh, sorry." She chuckled.

Ella sat there listening with her hands clasped in her lap as her nervousness got worse.

She had thought about the fighting, the demons, and the exorcism, but she hadn't thought about the danger. She hadn't thought about the fact that by returning to New York, she would be put on a team where people died long before the others.

She didn't want to be a redshirt. She wanted to go back to the main island and continue training.

These guys are seriously yanking your chain, Melneck assured her. *You are freaking out for no reason. It's just a damn shirt. There is no such thing as a jinx.*

I thought that about demons, too, Ella shot back. *But here I am with one inside me and many who want to kill me and eat my body.*

Relax. He chuckled. *Besides, you aren't the redshirt. This is your team's home base. Those two idiots across from you are the expendables.*

18

Katie sat down at the table in the main area of the base, looking over her shoulder at one of the other team members. He had just asked her on a date, and he hadn't been the first to do so.

Three guys had asked her out so far, and although she turned them all down, the phenomenon did intrigue her a bit. It was a surprise; she wasn't used to it. When she had been in college she'd gotten hit on all the time, but that was because she'd had a volleyball body and long flowing hair.

She had been surrounded by college guys then—back in what she called the "real world"—but she hadn't even been looked at sideways since she had become Damned. Even the cops in Los Angeles hadn't hit on her, although in all fairness they had been terrified.

"Hey," Katie murmured to Damian as he ate his sandwich.

"Yes?" He looked up at her.

"So, several of the guys here have hit on me." Katie leaned forward. "I'm not used to that. No one back home hits on me, like at all."

"Yeah, it was bound to happen." Damian smirked. "In Las Vegas they see you as a teammate, even more like a sister. These guys don't know you, which makes you fresh meat."

"Oh." Katie grimaced at the analogy.

She went back to eating her food and thought about what Damian had said. While she was very thankful that the guys on her team thought of her that way, she never had realized there might be a possibility of a relationship inside their world. Her mind went to Korbin and Stephanie and their more-than-obvious attraction. Maybe there was a possibility for more with them, which was something Katie felt they both needed desperately in their lives. Just as Korbin ran through her head her phone rang, and it was him.

"Hey, boss," she answered, licking a thumb and wiping it on her napkin.

"Is Damian with you?" he asked. The question produced a sinking feeling in her chest.

"Yeah." She swallowed hard.

"Put this on speaker," he directed.

"Damian." She nodded to the phone in the center of the table. "Okay, Korbin go ahead. We are here."

"I got an interesting email yesterday from the DEA," he started. "Attached were three videos from the bank in Los Angeles that you two decided to play superhero in. They have been squashed, but the two of you need to be more careful when you decide to go all vigilante. If these videos had spread you could have been outed, and that would be bad for all of us."

Katie didn't like being accused of playing superhero, but she understood the gravity of the situation—especially if those tapes had been released.

It was obvious from Korbin's tone that their identities had not been concealed at all. She started to think about her mother; about what it would have done to her to see her "deceased" child on a video fighting crime.

"Sorry, Korbin," Katie told him sincerely.

"It won't happen again," Damian agreed, glancing at Katie.

"See that it doesn't," he ordered, and disconnected.

Damian didn't say a word, just raised his eyebrows as he picked up his plate and walked away. Katie sighed and did the same, realizing that this was the first time in a week she had thought about her mom and her previous life.

Her brain hurt from it all, so she wandered around the house until she found the main TV area. It was empty and the lights had been dimmed.

She plopped down in a chair and pulled up the online archives of her soap opera. Pressing Play, she tossed the remote to the side and leaned her head back against the chair.

Before the opening credits had even finished, she heard someone enter the room. She lifted her head and looked over to find Ella in the doorway. She ran her hand down the doorframe and sauntered over, falling onto the couch. She propped her head up and looked at the screen and back at Katie, one eyebrow raised. Katie turned back to the soap and watched the show as the first scene played out.

Ella sat up on the couch and squinted at the television.

"I don't get what's going on," Ella complained. "And I don't understand why people even watch television anymore. Seriously, everything you would ever want to see is on YouTube. Sure, they've censored a lot of stuff lately, made it hard to watch full shows and movies, but if you have the money you can buy them on there too. Cable, in my opinion, is a complete waste of money."

Katie looked at her briefly and smiled, turning back to the show. Ella shrugged and sank back down in the couch, trying her best to follow the plot. It was ridiculous to her—a bunch of rich assholes and slutty women in weird love triangles.

"So, if she loves him and he loves her, why aren't they together?" Ella asked.

"That's Martin," Katie explained. "He is married to Melissa, but only because their fathers made them get married. They are both in love with other people."

This is fucking fascinating, Melneck told Ella. *Seriously, it's a total clusterfuck of humanity right there for the world to see...and I can't stop watching.*

Neither can I, Ella agreed, entranced. *It's like the worst train wreck ever, and you can't turn your eyes away. Do people actually live their lives like this?*

I don't know. Melneck scoffed. *It's been a while since I was last topside, but I sure as hell hope they do because this is the exact reason our kind is doomed to the flames. This, and your ridiculous shady-ass government systems...but that is a whole different topic.*

General Brushwood straightened his jacket as he leaned over the maps on his desk. Colonel Jehovivich stood by his side, waiting for him to speak.

They were back in their lair—or office—in the main headquarters of the military incursion base. Behind his chair was a large American flag, beside it the Army's, and on the other side a special flag designed specifically for their unit.

On the screen in front of them was a live feed of a group of men and women in military garb. They were gathered around a massive oak table in DC, ready to hear what the general had to say.

He was studying the map of the United States on his desk, on which red circles indicated the sites of the largest incursions. Next to him was a world map with the same markings.

He sighed and tapped his finger on Nevada. "There. That incursion in Nevada was the sixth-largest in as many weeks. With one major incursion taking place per week, we are being sorely tested by these demons. The events have increased by one major incursion per month just in the last three years. If you add in the demon who showed up in San Diego and then Los Angeles, these creatures are definitely upping their game—and at an alarming rate. All it will take at this point is for one major demon to be on the news and get shown all over the globe. That will provide the public with irrefutable facts we cannot deny, and our societies will uncover the truth about this secret war that we have managed to keep hidden for centuries."

"Sir, if I may speak freely?" Colonel Jehovivich requested.

"Go on."

"There have been numerous eyewitness accounts, including several sworn police statements, discussing a brand of weapon unrecognizable to the public," she explained. "These weapons are said to do more harm to demons than any weapon we possess—or that anyone else possesses, really. It is rumored that Korbin's Killers hold the weapons' patent, and that they have recently been handing them out to the teams. What, if anything, do you plan to do about this new weaponry?"

"At the moment?" He shrugged. "Absolutely nothing, to be honest with you."

"But sir..." The colonel stopped as the general shook his head.

"Look, it is obvious that they are trying to keep what they know to themselves," he continued. "If the government needs those weapons at some point, then the government will obtain them. I'm not above seizing them, just to make that clear. That being said, I would like to try using a little honey first. I don't want to make enemies of these people, and that is exactly what would happen."

Colonel Jehovivich nodded as the general turned to the screen in front of him.

"As much as I hate to admit it, there is a reason these mercenary groups exist," he began. "We don't have enough Damned on our teams to make a significant difference. We recruit anyone we can, but to be honest, those teams are capable of a lot more than we are at this point in time. They need to operate outside the military and political culture in order to do what they do. Recently the President signed off on an increase of more than fifty percent to our research division's budget. They are giving us the background we need to try to understand our enemy. This information is also pertinent because it offers us the possibility of taking the fight to them in the future—maybe even the near future."

"I'm sorry, sir." The colonel smirked. "Did you say 'taking the fight to them?' As in, taking our forces to hell?"

"That's where our military *always* ends up." The general glanced at her. "We go to Hell and back for the safety of this country."

Korbin picked up his cellphone, seeing Eric's name on the screen. The man was on the roof running security, but things had been quiet all day. They didn't think demons would come back to the base, but they weren't taking any chances. They wouldn't leave the compound unguarded until they could get everything transferred over to the new property. They were vulnerable here; out in the open, not disguised, not shielded—just sitting ducks for anything the demons might throw their way. It was anything but an ideal situation, that was for damn sure.

"How's it going up there?" Korbin asked.

Eric was lying on the roof with his sniper rifle propped on the parapet. He pressed his earpiece, directing the call through his headset while he squinted through the infrared scope into the distance. It was a dark night, but the sensors on his scope would show him any approaching heat signatures.

"I see what appears to be a gray wolf, sir," he told Korbin, looking at the animal's markings. "It seems to be alone, not in a pack like they usually are—though we don't see wolves around this area very often."

"A wolf?" Korbin asked. "I've heard that they have been creeping in, but all the way out here?"

"It could be a demon," Eric suggested.

"It could be, but I have never known them to have much interaction with that species. They are too wild and unpredictable," Korbin mused. "I could be wrong…and I don't want to be wrong about this, so snuff it. I'll take care of the reporting later."

"Yes, sir." Eric clicked off the call.

He leaned forward, watching the animal as it trotted across the desert with its beautiful gray fur blowing gently in the wind.

It reminded him of his dog back at home, the Husky that had been his first love. He shook the thought from his head, knowing that it wasn't healthy and would only make killing this animal that much harder.

Eric had seen people die; had shot people before, but he had never had to kill an animal, and for some reason the idea bothered him. He just wanted a sign, something that told him positively that the animal was a threat—and that was when he saw the flash of its red eyes.

Silly humans. The demon laughed. *They underestimate us all the time. Isn't that right, little poochie?*

The wolf's paws pranced through the warm sand as the demon inside him controlled where he went. The lights ahead would normally have scared the wolf off, but he was no longer in there; no longer controlling his own instincts. The demon, though relatively low-level, thought for sure he had found the key to success.

"You'll never do anything with your demon self." He snickered. *That's what they have always told me. I wasn't smart enough to kill a human, much less infiltrate the Killers' base. Ha! I'll show them. Sure, it was a little hard to wrestle this one down, but now I have the upper hand.*

The wolf stopped for a moment, squinting through the dark before starting to walk forward again. The wind blew from behind him, making it impossible to smell what was ahead. The demon didn't care, though. He found his vehicle of choice, one he thought would not be detected by the ignorant humans.

This time next week I'll be sitting in T'Chezz's office getting the accolades I deserve, he boasted to himself. *With these sniffing capabilities, the stealthy way it moves, and the ability to hear anything in the surrounding area, it's pretty much foolproof. I have this in the bag. I'll show them who the smart one is.*

The demon slowed the wolf down, then came to a stop in the sand. He tilted his head and looked at the compound, pricking his ears at the sound of someone moving. A red beam suddenly flashed out, rolling across the desert and up his body to stop right between his eyes.

Uh oh, the demon thought.

BOOM!

There was nothing left of the wolf's head, and the demon went straight back down to hell.

19

Katie pulled herself out of bed and yawned. The sun was not yet up.

She looked around the guest room they had put her in, which was smaller than her room at home but comfortable enough for her to get a good night's sleep. She wanted to get some training in, since she wouldn't have to work out in dust and debris like she had recently at home.

She washed her face and brushed her teeth before pulling on her normal black spandex pants and tank top and the gear they had provided her. As she laced her boots an alarm sounded, and lights began to flash in the hallway outside her room. She smiled and grabbed her knives, slotting them into her vest's sheaths.

Time to rock and roll, Pandora chirped.

Katie grabbed Ella, who surprisingly was already awake and dressed, and they headed down to the team area. When they arrived they joined Damian and the Jersey team at the side of the room, waiting for the team's second to appear. All were quiet, standing easily, geared up and ready to rock.

One of the Jersey team approached with some papers in his hands. "Busy morning," he told everyone. "We have two large events in New York City, and three smaller ones right here in New Jersey. I want two teams of two to go out on two of the incursion calls. I want the fifth man on this team to join them in the City to help out, and I would like Katie and Damian to take the last call here in Jersey."

"What about me?" Ella shouted.

"You will stay here and man the fort." He smiled. "You are not quite ready for this one."

Katie patted Ella on the shoulder and smiled, then caught up with Damian as he headed off to take the call.

Ella kicked at the floor, pushing her hands into the pockets of her sweatshirt and muttering to herself.

"I didn't want to go on no stinking incursion anyway," she grumped. She walked over to the doorway and watched the three teams racing toward the SUVs. She knew she would get her chance, but she couldn't help but be impatient. Fuck it…maybe she would just take a nap or something.

Meanwhile, Katie jumped in the SUV with Damian and inputted the GPS location. They took off out of the base and rolled down the road for about fifteen minutes. When they arrived, they pulled up outside the house in question and looked at each other suspiciously.

The house was obviously party central. There were beer cans throughout the yard, the front door was wide-open, and someone's boxers were hanging from the tree out front.

"Are those bodies?" Damian asked, pointing to the half-naked men face-down on the lawn.

"There's only one way to find out, I suppose," Katie grumped, opening the door and getting out.

She crept across the yard and looked around her, making sure there were no demons in the shadows. Slowly she bent down next to one of the guys and pressed her fingers against his neck. He was alive, and he smelled like he had drunk a keg the night before. She went to all three bodies and sighed, shaking her head.

"They are just drunk," she told Damian, disgusted. "Not a demon effort, just a seriously badass rager."

Ella whistled as she walked through the base, trying to get rid of the boredom. She was the only one left in the building, and they hadn't given her any tasks to take care of.

She thought about working out but passed, figuring no one was there to help her anyway. She went up the stairs to the top floor and down the hall, looking at the different paintings and pictures decorating the walls.

She stopped about midway down.

"Those Who Have Paid Tribute," she read out loud. "Huh."

There were rows of plaques, each with a picture, a name, a date (which she assumed was the date of their death), and some words of description. She reached forward and ran her fingers over the engravings, reading some of the stories underneath the pictures. This was the first time since she had gotten here that she was careful and thoughtful.

Some of the plaques—the ones in the top rows—had no pictures, and some of the names were only first names. The dates spanned over two hundred years. She hadn't realized how long humans had been fighting demons until that moment. When she reached the first picture she stopped, reading the information aloud.

"Ely Holmes, March 4, 1973," she read. "Ely was born and raised in Illinois and served in the military during some of the toughest battles in history. Ely became a Damned during his last tour in Japan, and joined the team voluntarily when he returned. During the Great Battle of the Plains he fought valiantly but was taken down by a Level-Seven, leaving behind only the memory of his bravery."

Shivers ran down her spine as she moved on to the next.

"Melissa Overland, June 11, 1999. Melissa was born and raised in the Deep South, playing in the bogs off the great Mississippi. She was the oldest Damned to join the team, starting at the young age of fifty-three. Melissa is accredited with taking down over three hundred demons before her death at the age of seventy-two. She was spry and witty, and her laughter will forever echo the Damned Hall of the Great."

She raised her eyebrows, picturing her grandmother kicking ass in a demon incursion. She chuckled to herself and moved to the end of the rows. There was one guy and one girl, the most recent deaths. She stared at the boy's picture, his blue eyes flashing like he was right there in front of her.

"Lyndon Ames, October 14, 2017," she read. "Lyndon had only been with the team for two weeks, but he showed the strength and honor of forty men. He led the team into a great battle and killed fourteen demons on his own before falling. His death was quickly avenged, and his body will ever lie at peace. He may have only been a whisper in the timeline of events to the Damned, but his legend will continue."

She shook her head. It all seemed so crazy, so wild, that these people had come and gone so quickly. She looked at the next plaque, a picture of a girl, not much older than Ella, her face innocent, her eyes wide, and her long brown hair cascading over her shoulders.

"Melanie Hanes, January 12, 2018," she read slowly. "Melanie came to the team as a wild and dangerous girl looking for her place in life. She found it with the Damned, learning, training, and fighting her way to the top of the ranks in record time. As the team heavy she maintained a strict code of always helping her teammates, no matter what the cost. That was how she died, protecting a teammate and saving their life. Melanie will forever be remembered for everything she was."

Ella took a step back and looked at what she had just read; two men, two women, all valiant, strong, and honorable, from different corners of the world, and all had given their lives for the same cause. Melanie had been just a year or two older than Ella when she died, and Ella took that straight to heart.

She could die too, and very easily—especially given where she was. Suddenly she wasn't so upset about being left behind.

Do you realize now why you need to train? Melneck asked.

Ella shook the sadness from her eyes and cleared her throat.

Of course, she barked. *I'm not an idiot. I just want to train in the afternoon! There's no reason to begin life before noon.*

Melneck chuckled, knowing those plaques had done more than any training she had received so far.

———

Korbin stepped out of the car and shielded his eyes from the sun as he looked around the property. It was the second time he had been there, but the first time he hadn't been able to check it all out. There was a two-story building that was probably the barracks Stephanie had described, and a small building next to a blackened launchpad. In the distance he could see some large concrete pads.

"So, there are two main underground buildings, and they are connected by a hundred or so foot long tunnel," Stephanie told him, giving him the specs. "The underground areas are reinforced concrete with eighteen-inchthick ceilings and walls, and a three-foot layer of earth above them. There's about fifteen thousand square feet of floor space, so we should have ample room. The control room is underground, and is about fifty by ninety feet with about forty-five hundred feet of floor space."

"How many acres, and is there water and such?" Korbin asked, looking around.

"Yeah, there are wells around the property, and the part you're interested in is a good thirty acres." Stephanie sighed. "The US government kept many of these bases a secret, so they could use them for other things."

"How did *you* find out about it, then?" Korbin asked.

"I had a couple of connections through my prior business." Stephanie smiled. "You would be surprised at the power that walked through those doors. Anyway, those connections led me to this place and they sold it to me for cash; no trace of its existence."

"Sometimes I think I just shouldn't ask." Korbin smirked.

"It's not like I paid for them in flesh!" Stephanie rolled her eyes. "Make the best out of every situation you find yourself in."

"Very true." Korbin shrugged.

"I know it looks overwhelming," Stephanie said. "But this place still has almost everything we will need. It just will require a team to get it fully operational. This will definitely not be a one-man show. Derek won't be able to handle all of it on his own, so you will want to think about who you can put in here to get things rolling. Of course, if you need help with that, you know I have resources."

"Right." He chuckled. "Though I don't know if the gangsters you brought in the other day would be able to figure out the IT logistics."

"Hey, they were just muscle," she protested. "Muscle that knows the importance of the word 'discreet.'"

"I hope so," he replied, walking forward to the edge of the launch building and scanning the land in front of him.

It was sand for the most part, but farther out there were both grassy and dirt-covered areas, with a ridge of short cliffs running along the edge. It was quiet—very quiet—and they could see for miles in all directions. There was a lot of work to be done, but he couldn't imagine the place not being perfect for what they were trying to do.

"Out there," Stephanie told him as she came up beside him. "There used to be a dirt airstrip. It was somewhere between twelve and fifteen hundred feet long, but it hasn't been used for nearly thirty years."

Stephanie pointed at a strip of grass and dirt to the west, which was overgrown but recognizable. Korbin put his hand to his chin, thinking about what it would take to make it useable again. He wanted an airstrip. It was a priority, but he knew that living quarters were first and foremost.

Stephanie and Korbin walked around the base, stopping at the concrete slabs with Joshua's machines on pallets stacked on them.

They could probably use those slabs to put up some new buildings on, or even possibly a kitchen where everyone could take turns preparing dinners and such. It was a long shot, but Korbin thought maybe it would be better than pizza every night.

Stephanie pointed to an area fifty or so feet away. "I want to create the foundation for the business, for Joshua's things, right beyond this slab we're standing on. It will connect to the network down below, though I don't think we will be able to put the machines below because of ventilation issues for now. Maybe in the future we can move everything down there and have him completely hidden away from the world. I think he'd much rather have it that way than have to run screaming every time someone came to the base. The more I'm here, the more I appreciate the usefulness of underground compounds."

"I don't know if that will be possible, actually," Korbin admitted. "As much as I would like to have him stowed away, I doubt that we will be able to put that part underground without risking our safety, due to the high gas content of the metals he works with. That being said, we can put the raw materials down below in a vault, along with the finished product. That will leave very little aboveground—maybe nothing more than the equipment and the work in progress."

"The finished weapons could be stored in the weapons bunker with the rest of them," Stephanie suggested. "Whatever is available for team use can be left out, and the rest can be locked up for clients and orders. If there gets to be too much stock to keep in there, we can always create a bunker just for those. There are plenty of areas underground. Even if we had everyone live underground instead of in the barracks, there would still be dozens of rooms available for us to use."

"Good." Korbin nodded. "Oh, and I forgot to tell you—I spoke with a contact at the airport. There is a MH-6 Little Bird for sale that I am considering purchasing. It won't carry the entire team—maybe five at the most—but I was thinking that would get us on the road a lot faster. I could get from here to the jet facility in Las Vegas in about fifteen minutes. I am still looking for a chopper that's big enough for the whole team, but I figured it would be a start. We can use it locally for reconnaissance. They are relatively straightforward to fly, too."

"That's awesome," Stephanie exclaimed, slapping him on the shoulder. "Get your airstrip set up and you are a bona fide operation."

"I sure hope so." He chuckled.

20

Katie kicked a red solo cup across the floor and went around the corner into the kitchen, where Damian was standing amidst bottles and mess. Given the party they had thrown the night before, there were bound to be some hungover twenty-somethings nearby besides the ones on the lawn. Unless they were infected twenty-somethings, though, the call was a complete bust. Damian held up a bottle of no-name whiskey and grimaced.

"They should be locked up."

"There's no evidence of anything demon-related here." Katie picked up a bra with the tip of her knife. "I'll call it in."

"Good idea," Damian agreed as Katie got on her phone. "And ask if anyone there wants some stale Doritos or Natural Light beer."

Katie laughed, turning away with the phone pressed to her ear. It wasn't the excitement she had expected, but at least they had found three living people and the humor of the situation. The phone rang twice, and the local lead picked up.

"This is Max."

"Hey, it's Katie. We are at 419 Brunswick. There's nothing here except the remnants of a party and three passed-out kids in the front yard."

"All right, good," he said, making a note. "We have another call. Write down the address."

"Okay," Katie said, pulling her notepad from her back pocket and grabbing a pen out of the puddle of beer on the table. "Hit me with it."

Katie and Damian left the party house and stepped into the SUV. One of the kids slowly raised his head off the grass to watch them drive away.

Katie chuckled as she put the address into the GPS. She sat back and looked out the window. She had never been to a party like that, not even in college. Between keeping her grades up to keep her tuition assistance and playing volleyball for a coach who monitored their every move, she had stayed out of fraternity row for the most part.

Most of the girls on her team had bitched about it, but Katie was fine. She wasn't interested in getting barfed on.

As they turned away from the main street, Katie realized that the scenery was changing with it. The houses were smaller and more run-down, and the general area wasn't very well-kept.

She got a chill up her spine, and realized that this one might be the real thing. Damian slowly pulled up in front of the target house and they got out, making their way to the door.

The yard was overgrown, and there weren't any signs of life. When they knocked on the door they heard low, deep growls, followed by the sounds of furniture crashing to the floor.

"What in the hell is going on in there?" Damian asked. "Sounds like a fucking twelve-foot Rottweiler."

It's no normal dog, Pandora warned. *Those are hellhounds.*

What? Katie replied, putting her hand up to signal for Damian to wait. *You guys can enter hounds?*

Well, yeah. We can enter pretty much anything with a soul, she explained. *But that isn't what is inside that house.*

Katie sighed. *Okay, then what's in there?*

Those are real hellhounds. Demons that look like very large dogs with vicious teeth, red eyes, and parts that would make your grandmother turn over in her grave.

"Oh, that sounds lovely," Katie said aloud, rolling her eyes and shaking her head.

"What?" Damian asked.

"Pandora said those aren't actual dogs," Katie reiterated. "They are—"

"Hellhounds," Damian interrupted. "Never actually seen one in person, but I've heard some really nasty stories. Interesting. New Jersey doesn't only have bad television shows, they have dogs that like to eat humans. I knew this place was a fucking armpit."

"I was always a cat person anyway," Katie said, sheathing her knives. "Though I'm not jumping on *that* train, because the next thing I know a demon lion will be chasing me down the street."

Actually— Pandora began.

I don't want to hear about it. Keep it to yourself, Katie snapped.

Fine, but if we go to Africa you are arming yourself with a fucking flamethrower, Pandora warned.

Deal, Katie replied. *It would be awesome to have one of those right about now.*

Katie and Damian looked at each other for a moment before simultaneously pulling out their pistols.

Katie let out a deep breath and reached for the door handle, not looking forward to this one. Damian nodded at her as she flung the door open and pointed her pistol inside.

Her face curled into a grimace. Inside—pretty much all over the living room—were the bits and pieces…of a family, they decided, since there were enough body parts to point to multiple people. Two hellhounds were curled up by the fireplace chewing on various body parts, and through a door they could see a third sprawled on the kitchen table, its eyes closed, apparently asleep. The two by the fireplace immediately stood, growling loudly, and dropped the bloody bits to the floor.

Katie ran in and Damian shut the door behind him, both pointing their pistols at the beasts. The first one lunged toward Katie, forcing her to dive to the side. It whimpered as it hit the wall, tearing the cables from the back of the television. It jumped to its feet and growled, narrowing its eyes and focusing in on Katie. She got to her feet and put her hands up.

"There, there, little puppy," she cooed, putting away her pistol and slowly pulling out her sword. "Be a good doggie and heel."

The dog barked so loudly the house shook before sprinting toward her at full speed. It leapt into the air and dove for Katie's head, its teeth shimmering in the light from the window. Katie screamed, slashing her sword through the air and taking the dog's head clean off its shoulders. The beast immediately evaporated into dust, showering her with its remains. She spat the ashes from her mouth and looked at Damian, who was wrestling the second hound on the floor. He had lost his pistol during the fight, so he couldn't just shoot it.

"This is no time for games," Katie said, marching over and kicking the dog in the ribs.

It snapped at her, almost taking off her arm. She pulled her hand back with wide eyes and growled at the beast. She sheathed her sword and grabbed both of her knives, jamming them into the dog's hairless back. It whined loudly and lifted its legs from Damian's arms. He quickly pulled a knife and slit the hellhound's throat, closing his eyes as the beast turned to dust.

"Jesus," he said, shaking the dust from his body. "Bad-fucking-Fido."

"Right?" Katie said, reaching down and helping him to his feet.

A moment later they heard a snarling growl behind them and they slowly turned toward the entrance to the kitchen, where the last hellhound was licking its lips and growling at them. It bolted toward them, forcing Katie and Damian to dive to the side. The beast kept going, breaking through the large glass window in the front wall and taking off down the street.

"I think that new Purina formula is really helping Spot grow," Katie remarked, looking out the window.

It was the Robertsons' fifth annual barbeque, and they had set everything up just perfectly.

Mrs. Robertson was inside making some Watergate Salad while the guests milled happily around the perfectly manicured lawn. Mr. Robertson stood at the grill wearing his "Best BBQ Dad" apron, spatula in hand.

Kids ran through the yard, giggling and screaming as they chased the family pooch, a chihuahua named Fifi. Mrs. Robertson stepped into the doorway and called all the kids inside to watch their favorite movie. The ten or so adults laughed as the kids bolted in, excited for another rousing viewing of the Disney classic.

"You should get yourself a bigger dog," one of the guests commented to the host. "Maybe something like a lab, or maybe a German Shepherd."

"I've been thinking about it, actu—"

He dropped the spatula as a huge horribly-disfigured and diseased-looking hound leapt over the six-foot fence around their yard. He scraped up the grass and dirt as he landed, and flung slobber all over the guests. They screamed and backed up as the beast looked right and left, trying to figure out where to go next.

Fifi ran forward and barked loudly at the hound. The hound looked at the other fence, but before leaping over he grabbed Fifi and chomped her in half, leaving the little dog's body on the grass.

Everyone was silent for a moment after that, but then they started screaming again, and grabbing one another. Mr. Robertson, his mouth hanging open, looked up as two people jumped his fence, landing right next to the half-eaten chihuahua. The woman looked down and grimaced, then glanced at the crowd, who quickly pointed to the adjacent fence. She smiled and nodded and they both took off again, hurtling that fence and disappearing.

The dumbfounded guest standing next to Mr. Robertson began to clap.

"Whew," he yelled. "That was some freaking show, man. I mean seriously, what are you doing to us here? You got a Marvel comics punk or something going on? Where are the hidden cameras? I bet there's one on that button on your apron."

He leaned forward at the button and smiled, waving wildly.

"That was really something," he said, patting Mr. Robertson on the back. "Hilarious, actually. Really funny. Where's your real dog? I mean, wow! They really are making those animatronic dogs lifelike now, aren't they?"

He walked over to the dog's back end and picked it up, whereupon half its intestines fell to the ground. He laughed and faked a scared face as the rest of the guests grimaced.

Mrs. Robertson walked to the doorway, wiping her hands and smiling, having missed the whole event. She froze, then let out a bloodcurdling scream.

"FIFI, MY PRECIOUS BABY!"

The guest dropped the bloody carcass.

The gray and white cat tiptoed across the privacy fence between the yards.

His tail was high as he sniffed the breeze that blew through the neighborhood, and he opened his mouth to sing the mating song of his people.

Peering out the window of the house next door was a very irritated man in his mid-fifties. He was wearing slippers, and his round belly hung over the top of his shorts.

"Oh Roger, just let it go," his wife said wearily, pushing her palm against her curlers. "It's just a cat."

"It's the Simmons' cat again," he hissed. "How many times do I need to tell them to keep that damn thing in their house? Not only is that wailing horrible to listen to, but he attracts all the other cats in the neighborhood and before we know it there's dirty cat pornography happening between our houses."

"It's just not worth going into it with them for the third time." His wife sighed. "You know they're going to keep that cat around."

"Yeah, well, I can fix this," he growled, turning and grabbing a shoe.

He slapped the sole of the shoe on his palm as he turned back to the window and put both hands on the frame to open it. However, when he looked outside, he dropped the shoe and slowly backed away from the window.

The hellhound bounded through yards, crashing through tables and just about drowning some people in a pool along the way. He ran toward a tall fence, tensing his muscles to jump it. As he did, he spotted a gray and white cat singing on top and leapt toward it.

He grabbed it in his mouth and chomped the little furball in half, dropping the pieces into the next yard. Up to that point, even though he had crashed through a number of backyards, he had attracted little attention.

He jumped another fence and took off across the street. Katie and Damian, who were following him, were panting from the exhaustion, so they stopped at the edge of the street to catch their breath. Katie looked at Damian and shook her head.

"Hellhounds really…*hate*…cats," Damian wheezed.

Katie nodded and they took off again, running through yards, jumping more fences, and untangling plants and bushes from their legs as they went. Katie leapt over another half a cat and shook her head.

"It's about time those animal control people got off their asses and did a little work around here," Katie yelled. "Stop leaving this shit for us!"

"Right?" Damian yelled back as they leapt over another fence.

They heard a yelp and looked at each other, then cleared the last brick privacy fence on the block.

When they landed they found the beast with its leg in the pool, licking its furless disgusting paw. Katie pulled out her sword and Damian his cross as they backed the snarling beast into the corner of the yard. Katie looked at

Damian and nodded, stepping forward with her sword in hand. She looked at the hound.

"Sorry, buddy, it's time to put you down," she told the thing as she swung the sword downward and split the dog's head in half. It turned into a pile of dust.

Katie leaned over and put her hands on her knees as an older woman walked out onto her deck and looked at them like they were crazy.

"My roses!" she cried.

"This is great fertilizer," Katie yelled back, dropping the handful of dust onto the ground. Damian laughed through his pain.

Ella had been at the base for hours on her own, with no idea when anyone was coming back. She had read almost every memorial plaque on the upstairs wall, and her nerves were on high alert.

Everyone was gone, and there was nothing keeping her there. She wanted to go home; to see her mom, hug her dad, and finally get her life together. She didn't want to be a demon slayer. She wanted to just be herself. She shook her head and grabbed her jacket as she walked toward the door.

Where are you going? Melneck asked.

I'm out, I'm done, she replied, slamming the door behind her and cutting across the front lawn.

Oh, hell *no,* he snapped, freezing her where she stood. *Not until we have a little talk.*

21

General Brushwood looked across his desk at Colonel Jehovivich. She shook her head and sighed, putting her cover down on the table. The general was quiet, thinking about the latest news to break across their desk.

"These military teams have got to get their shit together," the colonel said. "Excuse my language sir. I'm just tired of being in last place."

"I understand," the general said. "Your frustration is warranted, there is no doubt about that. I am feeling pressure from across the globe. The other countries are looking to us for support and guidance, and we can't even take out a little incursion in Middle of Nowhere, Minnesota."

"There has to be something we can do. The mercenary teams are great and they are carrying us, but there is only so much they can do with so few assets." The colonel sighed.

"Precisely," the general replied. "But right now, we are between a rock and a hard place."

"General Brushwood, Colonel Attlewood is here to see you. He says it's urgent," the secretary said over the intercom.

"Yes, send him in," the general directed, standing up and buttoning his coat. "We will continue this at a better time."

"Yes, sir," Jehovivich replied, standing up and nodding.

The door to the general's office opened and in walked Attlewood. He halted and stood at attention, and when the general nodded Attlewood walked forward in a hurry, carrying a folder in his hands. He nodded at Jehovivich and took a deep breath.

"There is a large demon incursion happening as we speak in Virginia, sir," he began. "We don't know how many or what size, but they are wreaking havoc. The team is ready to deploy, but they are requesting at least a two-person team backup from the mercenaries."

"Of course they are." The general sighed. "Let me make a call."

He went back behind his desk and opened his black phone book. He skimmed his finger down the numbers and stopped on John William Smith's name. If they were requesting mercenary backup the situation was bad, and he knew that the New York team could handle just about anything. He picked up the phone and dialed the number, looking at Jehovivich as she took a seat on the edge of the chair.

"John," he started. "It's General Brushwood."

"Sir," John replied. "What can I do for you?"

"There is an incursion in Virginia, and from what I've

been told it is a big one," he explained. "We have some men preparing to head out, but they are short-handed and are requesting backup. We are tapped out here, so I am calling to request that you send a couple of yours out."

"Okay." John thought for a moment. "I actually have a pair of redshirts who can go. They're from the Vegas base. They will need transportation. We don't have a chopper up here, and getting through New York airspace is almost impossible unless it's government."

"That's not a problem." The general looked at Attlewood. "We will send a Blackhawk to pick them up. What are their names?"

"Uh, Katie, who is the Las Vegas heavy, and Damian, their priest," John replied.

"Perfect. Tell Katie and Damian to be ready," he directed. "We are facing the possibility of a major incursion out there."

"They will want to bring their own weapons," John told him.

"They can bring the head of a chicken for all I care, as long as it will kill a fucking demon," the general replied.

"Yes, sir." John hung up.

It was going to be interesting.

"I don't think I've ever imagined something like that," Katie remarked as Damian drove them back toward the base. "I mean seriously, the thing was like a demon on steroids with a bone in his mouth."

"Did you see how he chomped that hole in the fence?" Damian chuckled.

"Yeah like he had a chainsaw for teeth." Katie laughed. "I have to give it to him…he bit that chihuahua in half like it was nothing. I really don't like those little yappers."

"Well, he's in chihuahua hell now, so you can rest assured the world is safe from another Taco Bell dog." Damian chuckled.

They pulled up in front of the base and hopped out, opening the back and grabbing their gear. Katie lifted her bag up and over her head, then stepped back so Damian could grab his stuff. They headed for the front door, but Katie stopped halfway up the walk.

"What is that?" Katie asked, slapping Damian in his stomach with the back of her hand.

"*What?*" He grabbed his belly. "You need to learn how to use your strength."

"Oh, sorry." Katie turned back to the yard. "That… Is that a *person* lying in the yard? Holy shit, is that *Ella*?"

They dumped their gear and raced across the yard, dropping to their knees at her side. Katie checked her heartrate, which was on the fast side of normal. She was out cold.

Katie looked at Damian, who had searched for wounds but found nothing. He shrugged in confusion and picked her up, cradling her in his arms. They made their way inside and down to the med bay, where he laid her on the table and began examining her further.

"I don't get it," Damian exclaimed. "There are no signs of struggle or injury or anything like that. Her vitals are all stable; the only thing odd is, her heart is a bit fast."

Just then she groaned, turned her head to the side, and fell silent again. Katie frowned and looked closely at the girl's face.

Pandora, can you tell if there is something wrong? she asked.

I already know, Melneck is restraining her, she told Katie.

"Melneck!" Katie called. "Let her go."

Katie shook her head and turned to Damian, who was looking at her strangely. Katie rubbed her temples and crossed her arms over her chest. She wasn't sure how to fix this, or even why it was happening.

"Her demon's name is Melneck," Katie explained. "He has her restrained."

"Why?" Damian asked.

"Who knows?" Katie replied. "She could be out for days."

Just then the demon released her, and Ella sat up and breathed in deeply. She started to cuss Melneck out as soon as she could speak, and her hands clenched into fists. Katie and Damian just watched her for a moment.

"That bastard froze me," Ella growled, looking at Katie.

"Why?" Katie asked. "What happened?"

"So…fucking…*stupid*. He thinks he can rule my life," she grumbled.

"Ella!" Katie yelled to get her attention before softening her voice. "Why did he restrain you?"

"I just wanted to see my mom, okay?" Ella screamed at Katie.

Katie clenched her teeth and slapped her across the face. Ella grabbed her cheek and gasped. Katie held her finger up and growled.

"Get over it," she yelled. "Don't get mad at your demon. He just saved you from becoming research!"

"What?" Ella whimpered, tears burning the corners of her eyes.

"I told you in the beginning," Katie reminded her, lowering her hand but sticking out three fingers. "There are only *three* options for people like us."

"Perhaps I wasn't listening," Ella confessed quietly, looking down at her lap.

"You think?" Katie growled, turning and pacing.

"You see, Ella," Damian said, stepping forward and checking her vitals again. "You can either die, become the lab's research subject, or work on the teams. There are no other options. Well, except for exorcism."

"What's wrong with exorcism?" Ella asked. "Why can't I do that? Get this lousy asshole out of me."

"It doesn't always work," Katie explained. "If your demon fights it and he is strong enough, which he is, it will mess you up really bad. You can end up in hell with your demon or be completely taken over by your demon—at which point we'll kill you—or even drop into a state of catatonia where you can't wake up but you can't sleep either."

"It seems worth it to me," Ella grumped, crossing her arms over her chest.

Sounds like you have a death wish, Melneck remarked calmly.

You don't like the idea of exorcism? Ella asked him. *You can be free of me, I can be free of you, and we can go our own separate ways, not even remembering each other. Life can go back to how it was...or it could be better, because now I can focus on school and stuff. We could get away from these people and back to our old lives.*

You would be back in your old life, Melneck pointed out. *I, on the other hand, would not.*

Why? Ella asked. *I don't understand.*

Look, there is no way I am leaving this side, he said. *And in an exorcism, I would have no choice. I know what is waiting for me back in hell, and that is not an option.*

What is waiting for you? Ella asked carefully.

The leader, or one of them. T'Chezz. He is trying to kill me, Melneck replied.

I thought you couldn't be killed? she queried.

I could be sent into the depths of hell, not to reemerge for centuries, or there are others—beings I don't wish to take notice of me—who might give me a permanent death. I'm told dying with you might accomplish that as well. And permanent death —just disappearing from life altogether, never coming back, poof, my dark and ominous soul lost forever—nope, not happening

Well, that sounds fun, Ella replied. *I mean, can't you fight him?*

"Oh, sure...fight a demon who has three times my power and a lust for torture and destruction? Melneck shot back. I don't think I would come out on top. So, stiff upper lip and all that, my dear. Tally-ho. My ass is going to stay right here in your body until he is dead or I can get away safely.*

"I hate my fucking life," Ella griped out loud, slamming her fists on the table. "Seriously, this is *my* body and *my* life. Why can't I make his dumb ass do what I want it to?"

Katie lifted her eyebrows. "I bet that was exactly what your parents wondered when you did it to them."

"I hate you, and I hate this fucking place," Ella grumbled. "I want to go home."

"You *are* home," Damian told her quietly. There was compassion in his voice. "Get used to it."

Damian looked down at his phone. John was calling him. He took the blood pressure cuff off Ella's arm and turned to Katie, holding up his phone. Katie nodded and came over, sitting down next to Ella. She tried to continue the conversation as Damian stepped out of the room and answered the phone.

"John. What's up?"

"A government chopper is going to be arriving, so you and Katie need to pack up," John told him. "You are headed to Virginia for an incursion with the military."

"Understood," Damian acknowledged and pressed End just as Katie walked up behind him.

He clenched his fists and gritted his teeth, shaking his head.

"Son of a *bitch.*"

"What?" Katie said startling him.

"Shit," he replied whirling around. "The government is coming to pick us up to go on a raid with them."

Katie stared at him. "I don't understand. What does that mean? I've never been on one before."

"Well," Damian growled, putting his phone back in his pocket, "usually it means that One, we get to be told what to do. Two, they are never in the right place at the right time to help us. Three, our butts are on the line. Four, they don't have any Damned on their teams. Five, we are the ones who get stuck on the front part of the spear. Six, it just continues to get worse, and seven, should anything work well they will get all the credit. Everything else is on us."

"*Fantastic.*" Katie sighed.

When the chopper arrived, Katie and Damian were already on top of the building waiting for them. They ducked as they ran forward, climbing in and taking the headsets from the pilot. They sat down on the floor in the back and braced themselves as a support person shut the doors and the chopper climbed into the air. Katie looked at Damian and shook her head. They couldn't even fly to Virginia in a damn seat.

"I am Warrant Officer Thomas. I will be flying you to the site," the pilot told them over the headset. "It shouldn't take long to get there. There will be a strike team of four there to meet you, and your commander on site will be Sergeant Michael McKay."

"Thank you," Damian replied loudly into the mic.

The pilot flipped some switches on the dash above him and rose higher into the air, flying quickly away from their Jersey base.

Katie held on tightly, looking out the plastic windows and wondering exactly what kind of hell they were in for.

She had always been good at following orders as a civilian, but once Damned she was less compliant. She hated taking orders from assholes who had no idea what they were doing. She hated taking orders from *anyone* anymore, but that was just her demon talking. She knew that, because she greatly respected Korbin...and John, for that matter.

They were true leaders; always informed, never missing a beat, and fighting for their team every step of the way. Katie appreciated them, because she knew that if she had to answer to the higher-ups she would be research in a heartbeat.

When they landed the soldiers were standing in the tall grasses holding their helmets on and clutching their M16s in one hand. The sergeant was standing tall at the front with a smug look on his face.

Katie rolled her eyes, knowing exactly what kind of guy he was before she even exited the helicopter. She was not going to walk his walk, that was for damn sure, and if he wanted her help, he was going to have to damn well earn it.

She climbed out of the chopper and ducked until it disappeared into the sky. Katie and Damian walked quickly over to the sergeant.

"Sergeant McKay," he introduced himself. "The building to your left," he pointed like she couldn't figure out what the hell he was talking about, "is the one in question. Three cops were originally called out for 'funny noises,' and they are now down. There are more police here, but they will not be engaging. From there...well, we have found ourselves a large group of possessed, and none of them seem salvageable."

"'Salvageable?'" Katie repeated, turning to Damian, who shushed her and shook his head.

She already didn't like this guy. He was a know-it-all who liked being in charge, and in order to separate his feelings from his duty he referred to people as "salvageable" or not.

Like they were old fruits and veggies in the back of the fridge that he was trying to decide whether to throw out. It was a disgrace…but at the same time, none of these guys were Damned. None of them knew the trauma and the trials that people like Katie and Damian and the rest of the teams went through on a regular basis.

He and his team could do their jobs and go home to their families at the end of the day.

"The cops have the place locked down," McKay informed them as they walked toward the building. "There is a perimeter around the building, and all the streets are completely blocked. Air travel has been suspended for five miles around the building, so there is no chance of the press getting wind."

"Okay." Katie wanted to say something about priorities, but bit her tongue. She really didn't give a shit about the press when there were lives at stake, but she tried to understand it was part of his job.

"We go in, we do our jobs, and we come out," McKay said to those assembled. "Katie, Damian, you're Team One. Work the demons between us and the end monster. They always have end monsters, right?"

Damian and Katie rolled their eyes, although they

looked at the ground first. What a complete moron. Katie wondered if this guy had ever even faced a demon before, much less led a group of unsuspecting soldiers into the middle of an incursion.

"Yeah, sure," Katie mumbled. "Just like a video game— boss man at the end of the level. Maybe we'll even find a magic mushroom to eat and grow bigger."

Damian elbowed Katie and smiled, holding his laughter in. Luckily none of the others noticed their taunting. Damian could barely keep the smile off his face. Katie knew this was going to be one hell of a ride with this idiot in charge.

She didn't know whether to be scared for them or to feel like she had won the fucking lottery with this asshole.

She was going to go in there with all guns blazing and show them a thing or two about fighting demons, that was for damn sure. None of them, including Captain Crunch there at the front, were going to be the same when they came back out.

"So, wait…I just want to make sure I have this straight," she said to McKay. "You know, just to be on the same page as you valiant soldiers."

"Okay." He smiled, not catching her sarcasm.

"Your strategy is that we," she waved a finger between herself and Damian, "me and my partner, kick everything's ass until the end. Then you guys roll in, fresh as fuck, and take on the bad boss-guy to level up?"

Damian cleared his throat, trying to hold back new laughter. He had a sudden desire to look the other direction.

"Yep, though I'm not sure what leveling up means,"

McKay replied. "Must be a mercenary term. But sure…you guys roll in ahead of us, so we are ready to take on the big guy. Then we can give you a little break while we take him down and tie up the loose ends. We wouldn't want to send the two of you into the boss and endanger your lives any more than we have to."

"No, no of course not," Katie agreed, nodding her head.

"All right, team, let's make sure our vests are secure and our eyes are peeled," McKay ordered, clapping his hands.

Damian grabbed Katie by the arm and led her off to the side, covering his mouth with his clenched fist. As they walked toward the front door of the building Damian took a deep breath, still trying to stifle his laughter.

Katie shook her head. She still didn't believe the shit they got into on a regular basis.

"So," Damian clarified, "they get all the glory for taking down the 'boss,' and then receive the highest payout for the biggest demon. They are playing us hardcore, and that sergeant *knows* it."

<hr>

Ella walked through the base house and out to the front balcony. She sat down and looked out over the New York City skyline. She used to climb to the top of her parent's apartment complex almost every morning after a long night of drinking and watch the sun shine through the different glass buildings as it rose. It looked different now; almost more realistic than before.

Why so glum? Melneck asked.

I just don't know how to get used to this, she told him. *I* mean, I'm never going to be alone again, I can't go out, I can't see my parents, and everything I ever wanted to do has been squashed.

You need to start looking at the world differently, he suggested. There is a huge difference between positive and negative. Though it may seem all these things are negatives in your life, they don't have to be.

Right. She scoffed. And how can I see differently?

Well, from being in here I have learned that before you always felt alone and you only went to those parties and things to be surrounded by people, he explained. Now you don't need that part, because I am here to kick your ass.

Great. She rolled her eyes.

You miss your parents. I'm sure that sucks, but it is what it is. You have freedom now, and that is a positive, he continued. And as far as your dreams for the future... Well, change them. Make them center around a world where you will have money, no identity, and the ability to do almost anything you want. There is no reason you can't take a vacation and see the world. You will be a badass bitch, and from what I hear, badass bitches are in high demand. You always wanted to be someone impor-tant, so here is your chance.

Yeah, maybe, Ella said doubtfully. Maybe you're right. I mean, people die all the time, and instead of it being my parents it was me— at least to them. I can know they are safe and secure without going through the hell that they put me through on a regular basis.

Yep, Melneck agreed. That is exactly right. And when all is said and done I'll let you exorcise me, and you can do whatever you want after that. For now, just enjoy being a badass bitch for a while.

Melneck? Ella asked.

Yeah?

Can I go to the store down the street? she asked. *I really want to buy a bottle of water and some fruit chews.*

Yeah, sure, why the hell not? But if you beat feet I'm freezing you again, he warned.

Yeah, yeah. She chuckled. *No fucking privacy.*

Ella headed downstairs and grabbed her bag, figuring there was no one there to tell anyway. She pulled her hood up over her head and shoved her hands in her sweatshirt pockets, walking alone through the neighborhood.

It was the Greek District so there were families everywhere, but she just didn't feel like looking at any of them. As she turned the corner, she walked past a school. There were kids out and about, playing sports, talking, and hanging out in the parking lot.

At first she didn't even look over at them, remembering how torturous her high school days had been, but as she passed them she heard a kid telling someone to get off and leave him alone.

She slowed down and watched as some bullies picked on a smaller, thinner boy. He didn't have the most fashionable clothes or the newest shoes, his haircut was like a bowl, and his glasses were broken on one corner. Below his feet his books were strewn everywhere, pages flapping in the breeze.

Those stupid motherfuckers, she grumbled to Melneck. *I fucking hate bullies. Why can't they find something better to do with their time?*

I don't know why you are bitching to me, Melneck replied. *You could be handling it right now. Why are you hesitating?*

I'm a girl, and I'm much smaller than those guys, she explained.

Seriously, I wonder if you are awake half the time when you are with everyone else, he mused. *You aren't paying attention to anything the Damned are trying to tell you, are you?*

I am, but I don't know what you mean, she replied.

Your practicing and training is what helps me adjust to you, he explained. *I can't help you in fights and I can't help you against demons if our bodies aren't aligned in some way or another. We have to do things like this to get more in sync. Now, just trust me this one time and go over there...*

23

Ella took a deep breath and walked toward the kids. When she reached them she pushed one of the big ones off the smaller kid. "Move it, asshole!"

They all stepped back, whistling and chuckling, Ella stood between them and the kid, fists clenched and jaw tight. She looked at the kid and then back at them.

"Leave him alone." She flicked her hair out of her eyes.

"Uh oh, look at the big girl," the leader of the boys taunted, cracking a smile to the others. "What, you just get out of school yourself? Think you are an adult and everything? I bet you are the type of girl who does everything your parents want you to. You trying to look tough with that streaked hair and goth makeup? It isn't working!"

Bwahahaha! Melneck laughed. *Boy, this kid has it all wrong. Not only do you despise authority, but you do the complete opposite of what your parents tell you. What an idiot! No, you fool, she is much worse than you could ever imagine.*

Shut the hell up, Ella yelled at Melneck. *I'm not that bad.*

You are right. He sighed, then started to laugh again. *You're worse! You are the stain on the bottom of a condom when the guy decides to watch two dogs getting it on rather than sleep with you! You are the reason there are only three people trying to console your parents. You sucked so bad as a daughter most people are congratulating them!*

I swear, if you don't shut up... Ella warned him.

You'll do what? He chuckled. *You are the worst example of human flesh I've ever been inside, and trust me—I've done this plenty of times. There are sloths that work at a higher level than you. In fact, I've met mental patients who have a better ability to function and stand up for themselves.*

"Stop," she shouted, her temperature rising.

Aw, am I hurting your wittle feewings? Is wittle Miss Ella gonna run home and cry? Or are you going to stand up like a true fucking demon fighter and do your goddamn DUTY?

The soldiers watched as Damian pulled out his large glimmering cross, holding it tightly in his fingerless-gloved hand.

They noticed that Katie's weapons were special as well, the blades of her knives shimmering in the dim light as she ran them effortlessly across the throats of the demons just inside the door.

When the blade touched flesh, it sizzled and crackled. Like individual tornados Damian and Katie whirled through the building, beating the shit out of everything that got in their way. While Damian blocked Katie kicked, sending demons flying backward in a ball of dust or blood.

They made their way through the halls in a dance of death with knives, crosses, punches, kicks, blocks, and bullets. It was the most amazing thing any of the military team had ever seen, and at the end of the cleared hallway— or rather, at the end of a trail of demon carcasses and piles of dust—was the room where their boss resided.

Katie and Damian stopped outside the door as the sergeant marched through their debris, with his three men shuffling clumsily behind him. When he reached the door he cleared his throat, obviously nervous but trying to hide it.

He looked at his men, then at Katie and Damian.

"We got this," he told the redshirts. "Good work."

Katie shrugged and stepped to the side as the men ran into the room. She skipped over to a couple of wooden containers against the wall, hopping up and patting the one next to her for Damian. He smiled and climbed up, groaning as he wiped off his cross and stuck it back in the inside pocket of his coat.

Katie smiled. "So, how is life? What do you think the new base is like? Meet any cool priests lately?"

"Well," Damian paused to let the sudden screams from the other room die down, "I am hoping there is a big place for a sanctuary, and a—"

A loud roar followed by rapid gunfire and further screaming made him pause again.

"Big room for me to relax in," Damian finished. "How about you?"

"I am hoping for a place I can make my own donuts," Katie told him. "Save me a lot of money."

"Ha-ha. I'm—"

They paused as one of the men came flying back through the door, landed on the ground and slid all the way to their feet. Katie looked down and shook her head in disgust, not understanding how they could possibly be screwing this one up.

She looked at Damian and they both nodded, then jumped down and picked the military guy up by his arms and legs.

"We'll just clean this up," Katie murmured as the two of them tossed him back through the door into the fight. She yelled after the soldier, "No lying down on the job!"

He screamed as he landed on his ass and skidded to the demon's feet. She flinched and then smiled, dusting off her hands and walking back over to the crate. They hopped back up and continued their conversation.

"Now, what was I saying?" Katie asked.

"Donuts," Damian reminded her.

"Oh yeah." She smiled. "So, I want to make my own donuts."

About two minutes into the conversation Damian paused, hearing only silence now from the other room. Katie tilted her head and waited until someone yelled from the other room.

"COVER FIRE!"

The three guys ran back out, carrying their fearless leader and laying him on the ground. He was out cold, but still breathing; no fatal wounds, just knocked the fuck out. Katie raised one eyebrow and looked at one of the soldiers, who was covered in dirt and breathing heavily.

"We're tapped out," he told her, clutching his chest.

"Oh, *hell* no!" Katie jumped down and putting up a hand. "Just because your leader is out cold, that doesn't mean you get to leave. He told me that you guys are the specialists. That you had this."

She waved them toward the room. "Go ahead. We got all night."

They looked at her pleadingly, and just then General Brushwood and Colonel Jehovivich barreled down the hall. The soldiers stood at attention and saluted as they waited for him to approach.

The general saluted back when he reached them.

"At ease," he commanded, staring at the sergeant on the floor and then at one of the soldiers. "I need a sitrep."

"Um, well, he," the soldier said, pointing at the sergeant on the floor, "decided that we would take out," he jerked his thumb back at the demon, "the boss demon there."

The general grunted in irritation. "Well, don't make me wait. What happened?"

"Well," the soldier answered, grimacing, "we got our asses handed to us."

A deep laugh tumbled from the room behind them, and the soldier lifted his shoulders and scrunched his face.

"Did all my toys leave me?" the boss demon voice bellowed. "Are none willing to play with Bokorgh?"

Ugh, it's Bokorgh. Pandora groaned. *He is a big one but a bit of a pussy, for what it's worth. Just watch out for his right cross. It will lay you out until next week.*

The general turned and stared at Katie and Damian,

who had their hands in their pockets. They hadn't even broken a sweat.

"What?" Damian asked. "We already did the rest of this."

Damian waved his hand at the hallway behind them. The general followed his gesture and watched as another of the wounded demons burst into dust. His mouth opened, but no words came out. He couldn't believe these two had done the whole thing.

"You want us to take out the last one too?" Damian asked with a smirk.

The general turned to the men, who nodded and shrugged.

"The sergeant told Team One—those two," the soldier confirmed, nodding to Katie and Damian, "to clean out the building so we could go in fresh."

"Let me get this straight," the general said slowly. "Your sergeant allowed these two fighters to go in and clean up the warehouse so, and I quote, you could, 'go in fresh.' And now your sergeant is laid out here unconscious, and you want the two demon hunters to go in there?"

The leader of the group just shrugged, not really knowing what to say. The general sighed and rubbed his face as he looked at the colonel. A loud bang shook the room behind them and the general flinched, rolling his eyes. He turned to Damian.

"Would you please finish this?" the general requested.

Damian and Katie nodded, stepped over the sergeant, and headed toward the door. Katie stretched her arms over her head and cracked her knuckles, then tilted her head quickly from side to side. She cleared her throat and kicked open the door, Pandora's voice joining with hers.

"Welcome to the jungle, *BITCHES!* We got fun and games coming your way!" she screamed.

That was when all hell broke loose.

The general stood next to the colonel and the other soldiers as Katie and Damian disappeared into the room. They could hear Katie and Damian fighting hard and taking blows, then the high-pitched screaming of the demon. The general looked at the colonel with furrowed brows, and she just shrugged. Suddenly Katie crashed through the wall and rolled across the ground toward the soldiers. They backed up as she jumped to her feet, not even noticing them as she talked to herself.

"Oh, you did NOT just throw my ass through a wall, you motherfucking irredeemable barrel-jacker!" she growled, clenching her fists.

The soldiers took another step back, looking at each other in wonder. This woman had just been thrown through a cinderblock wall, and she had gotten back up for more.

They had never seen anything like it. They were blown away and scared at the same time, so they just watched the action like birds watching a cat that was stalking something else.

Katie dusted off her pants and ran back inside, and they all stood there waiting for whatever would happen next. Sure enough, only a moment passed before the demon screamed again and there was a giant crash.

Before they could even blink the demon smashed through the wall, destroying part of the building. The soldiers and the officers ran for cover, leaving the sergeant where he was. They watched from behind the crates as

Damian and Katie stalked out of the room, their eyes on fire as they grabbed the demon by his legs and pulled him back into the other room.

The demon was gibbering in fear and clawing at the ground as they dragged him over the debris. The soldiers' eyes grew wide when Katie kicked him hard in the leg.

"Stop it," she yelled. "You're embarrassing the whole demon race! You could at least die with a little dignity. Damn, she was right when she said you were a pussy. You need to get it the fuck together. You did this to yourself."

A few minutes later another scream rang out, only this was worse than any of the others. It shook the walls, and forced the soldiers to put their hands over their ears.

After a few seconds it stopped, and perfect silence ensued. The military people crouched in the quiet, waiting for what was next.

To the right of them a piece of the ceiling crashed to the ground, startling them.

The general stood up straight and dusted off his uniform, then slowly inched forward and stared into the dust cloud ahead of him. He was pretty sure that the demon was dead. He looked down when he felt someone pulling on his pantleg. It was the sergeant, who had just woken up from his unconscious state.

"Did we take him out?" he asked, then closed his eyes again.

I would fucking kill *for a donut right now,* Pandora snarled.

I thought you were off donuts, Katie remarked, brushing the dust off her pants.

Donuts are a lover that you get into fights with, Pandora explained. *All so that you can have great makeup sex, but then you feel bad about yourself when you're done.*

Katie was confused. *So, are you telling me that you're giving up donuts?*

Which part of "you're talking crazy" don't you understand?

24

*Y*ou really can't see it? Melneck laughed. *You can't see how pathetic you really are?*

Stop it, Ella growled.

I mean, I thought I was blind to reality sometimes. He chuckled. But this? I mean, I saw it before I even entered your body. There you were, standing on those stairs, holding onto that little bag of trash, angry at the world. Poor Ella! She has to work a real job, and her parents give her a hard time. Boo hoo. Why don't we just run off and get high, because that solves everything? Please! Get it together here and face the cold hard truth. If you ever want to be anything in this world, you are going to have to install a new fucking brain.

"I said *SHUT THE FUCK UP,*" she screamed out loud, and the boys stepped back and looked at each other in confusion.

Yes, yes! That is it, right there, Melneck told her. Now you are ready! Tap it, feel the rage, BE the bitch you were meant to be. These boys are everything in the world you hate. They are your parent's nagging mouths, they are the demons around you, they are society's hold on you. This is your moment, now GIVE IN TO IT!

Ella lost it. She lunged forward and grabbed the leader by his shirt with one hand and punched him repeatedly in the face with her other hand. When she finally let go, he fell into a pile at her feet.

The next kid's fist hit her face, but there was no pain.

"That all you got, prick?"

She growled and grabbed him by the shoulders, ramming her knee into his gut before punching him hard in the side of the head and sending him spiraling to the ground.

She turned, thrusting her leg out to the side and kicking an oncoming guy in the chest. He doubled over and fell backward, wheezing as he landed on the asphalt.

"Behind you," the nerdy kid yelled, and she turned right into a punch in the mouth.

Ella spat and chopped the fourth guy in the side of the neck, then punched him in the stomach. Not content, she grabbed him by the shoulders and threw him to the ground. The leader had gotten back up and came toward her, screaming at the top of his lungs. She bent down and punched him square in the nuts, then stood up quickly and elbowed him in the neck. The fifth guy ran toward her as well, but she stepped to the side and stuck out her arm, catching him in the throat. He bounced backward and hit the ground, not getting up again.

"I...uh...I think you got them all," the kid told her, clutching his notebook to his chest as he looked around. He pushed up his glasses a moment later.

Ella stood up straight and glanced over as one of the guys tried to get up.

She walked over and tilted her head to peer at him, then pulled her leg back and kicked him hard in the stomach like she was punting a football. He collapsed again, out cold.

Her face was on fire, but she didn't care. She had kicked all their asses. She wiped the blood from her nose and mouth on the back of her arm.

She slowly walked over to the leader, who was groaning as he lay on the ground looking up at her. As she stared down at his pathetic face, she felt strong, powerful, and in control.

"Be thankful I don't hang your testicals around my neck like my friend told me I should do," she whispered to him.

Ella turned around and looking at the kid, who jumped slightly. She forced a smile, blood covering her teeth. He grimaced back as she walked over to him and patted him on the shoulder.

"If these assholes harm you again—make fun of you, hell, even breathe in your direction—I want you to let me know," she told him. "Next time I'll start my necklace."

"B-b-but I don't even know who you are," he stuttered. "How can I let you know?"

"I'm the new kid on the block," she replied. "I'll be around, don't you worry, and I've got your back."

Okay, cool girl, time to walk away, Melneck suggested.

Ella smirked and walked back past the guys lying on the ground. She pretended like she was going to kick one of them, and laughed when he flinched.

She marched back to the sidewalk and kept walking,

not knowing at that point whether to go back to the base or head to the store covered in blood. She didn't feel any pain anymore, and when she ran her fingers over her lips they were healed.

Melneck chuckled. *I never said to use their testes for a necklace.*

I know. Ella smiled. *I added that. You are too much of a pansy to say something like that.*

And I know how it feels to be punched in them, he added.

Now who's the big bitch? she asked, chuckling.

As she passed a car on the street she looked at her reflection, and she realized she couldn't go into the store covered in that much blood. She sighed and headed back toward the house. She slowed down and looked over her shoulder.

John William Smith was watching her every move from a distance. He nodded and stepped back behind the fence.

"You will do, little girl. You will do."

Why are you slowing down? Melneck asked. *People are starting to stare.*

I thought I saw someone watching me. She shrugged. *Guess I'm just paranoid.*

Let's talk about that kick, Melneck said. *I think you could use some help on the technique.*

Oh Lord, here we go. She sighed, rolling her eyes. *Nag, nag, nag... It's like having a grandma in my head.*

Hey, it's my job to help you get better,' Melneck replied. *And if you think that's nagging, you just wait until the Vegas kids are gone, I'm going to be your only friend.*

Right, because no one else will want to be my friend. She scoffed. *You are a forced friend; a leech I can't get rid of.*

A powerful one, Melneck reminded her.

A powerfully damned annoying one, Ella shot back with a smile.

The two argued as they walked back toward the house.

She might have changed in that high school parking lot, but things didn't change in her head.

Katie sighed as she shoved her things in her bag. Before she left, she checked the room one last time to make sure she hadn't forgotten anything.

It was time to head back to Vegas and get settled into to their new routine.

They would be moving to the new base soon, and she had a lot of shit to pack. Besides, she missed her room, she missed her team, and she missed normal demons without tails and snouts. She had to admit, though, it had *definitely* been an experience.

She walked out of the room and out to the sidewalk, where the team had gathered. She and Damian would take a car to the airport, where John had a jet waiting to take them home.

The other team members hugged her, some still flirting, then she went to the SUV where Damian, Ella, and John were waiting for her. It was in that moment that she realized she was going to have to say goodbye to the little one.

She had gotten kind of attached to Ella's snide attitude, bad jokes, and terrible sense of fashion.

Damian turned to Ella and smiled.

"Man, you look a bit the worse for wear there, priest,"

Ella commented.

Damian reached up and touched the bandages on his face. The last few cuts and scrapes had yet to heal. John and the others had taken very good care of them when they returned, and they had all sat around laughing at the story they told. John agreed that it sounded just like one of those ignorant assholes.

"Yeah," Damian said to Ella. "I haven't quite healed yet. While my demon is pretty good at the healing thing, I didn't get the same upgrades," he jerked a thumb toward Katie, "as this one."

"Hey, I saw the bloody mess Ella was when we got back yesterday," Katie exclaimed. "But today she magically doesn't have a scratch on her. Pretty impressive."

"Take care of yourself, kid," Damian said, hugging Ella.

She went rigid at first but slowly relaxed, leaning her head on Damian's shoulder and smiling. He ruffled her hair and stepped out of the way so that Katie could approach.

Katie walked up to Ella and blew out a deep breath of air, feeling slightly emotional about the entire thing.

"Don't let these guys push you around too much." Katie smiled at her and winked at John. "And remember…you are important, and you are one badass bitch."

"Melneck said the same thing." Ella smiled.

"Oh yeah?" Katie nodded. "You guys getting along better now?"

"Yeah," Ella replied. "Kind of. I mean, he showed me something yesterday; brought out a side of me that I didn't know I had. I think there might be some possibilities in our relationship. Probably not like you and yours have, but he definitely has his own interests at heart, which helps me become more of a badass. He's still a jackass, though."

Bitch, Melneck interjected. *Tell that human to tell her demon I'll be watching for her brother.*

"Oh, and he just said to tell Pandora that he will be watching for her brother," Ella relayed.

"Good." Katie nodded. "And when he finds him, I want to get in a few blows too. He stole my damn car."

Ella looked confused and Katie shook her head. "Never mind, not important. Come here and give me a hug."

Katie pulled her in and hugged her tightly, which gave her a warm sensation in her chest. She felt like Ella had become her little sister, and there was no doubt she was going to miss her—even if she *was* a pain in the ass.

Ella pulled back and quickly wiped a tear from her cheek, trying to hide her emotion. Katie rubbed the top of her head. Ella walked over to the guys and started joking around with them. Katie smiled and turned to John, who looked at her sweetly.

"I didn't get to take you out to dinner."

"I was too busy chasing hellhounds." She laughed. "Maybe next time."

"Definitely," John agreed.

"And hey…look out for Ella. She's a good kid underneath that tough exterior." Katie smiled. "I'm worried that she isn't ready, but I know she has what it takes."

John looked down at Katie and nodded in agreement. He knew she had what it took; he had seen it with his own eyes. Katie read the look on his face and smiled, nodding back at him before climbing into the SUV.

Feeling at ease, she waved at Ella as they drove off.

25

Katie looked at Damian, who had his head pressed against the glass and was breathing heavily, off in a dream world. She smiled and looked out her own window at the clouds. Her trip to New York—and Virginia, for that matter—had been eye-opening.

She had learned things about herself. She had learned things about other people too, realizing that everyone was going through their own inner struggle.

Watching Ella had made her remember all the emotions she had felt when she first joined the team, and she had realized how far she had come since then.

In the grand scheme of things it hadn't been that long since she had become a Killer, but she felt like a completely different person. When she got home she would embark on the next chapter, finding a new place to get comfortable and continuing to kick demon ass.

Speaking of a new place to live, she unbuckled her seatbelt and made her way to the front. She knocked gently on the cockpit doors and waited for the pilot to open it. He smiled as he took his seat again.

"Everything okay?" he asked.

"Yeah, I was just wondering if you could fly us over the new place before going home. I haven't seen it yet," she asked.

"Sure thing! We'll be coming up on it in about ten minutes."

"Perfect," she replied, then left the cockpit and made her way back to her seat.

Katie looked out the window in excitement as the plane broke through the clouds and he circled the new compound. She could see the whole place. There was a hell of a lot of land, and not much road. Part of it was desert, just like her old place, but part of it was dusty dry land with randomly-sprouting grasses. She leaned back in her chair and smiled, tapping her fingers on her lips.

Okay, Pandora demanded, *spill it. What are you thinking?*

Huh? Katie smirked. *I don't know what you mean.*

Come on. Pandora groaned. *I know that look, and you never tap your fingers on your lips if you aren't making some devious plan.*

Uh, devious is your *forte.* Katie laughed. *And it's nothing dubious. I was just thinking about the car.*

Oooh, Pandora exclaimed, excited. *I almost forgot that you owed me a car. What are you thinking...Aston Martin? Another Ferrari? What?*

Actually, I was thinking that there is a whole lot of land out there, Katie told her. *And maybe, just maybe, we are due for an upgrade.*

An upgrade? From a Ferrari? Pandora exclaimed.

Yup, Katie said, smiling. *Maybe something a little more appropriate for the terrain we are moving to. Something with a kick, that fits our style.*

Korbin, Stephanie, and Katie sat around the conference room at the old base talking about the Damned. Korbin wanted to know all about the trip: the details, how they ran things, and especially, to Katie's confusion, the military escapade. She told him what she knew: that they were idiots, how they had almost gotten themselves killed, and what had happened when the general had shown up. Korbin was not looking forward to talking to the general again, although he was sure they would be having a conversation soon now that they'd seen the weapons in action.

"Interesting," Korbin murmured. "And John didn't say anything about it?"

"I mean, he rolled his eyes and said that seemed to be typical military," Katie replied. "But other than that, no. He seemed to hate the whole part of the job that had to do with them."

"Right," Korbin said, sitting back. "Thanks. And I appreciate you keeping Pandora under wraps. It's going to be a difficult enough conversation when I have to explain the new weapons."

I'd like to wrap him, Pandora purred.

Katie ignored her and smiled. "No problem, boss."

"Okay, so back to what I was saying." Stephanie leaned

forward. "I am telling you, I have intel on who the infected humans might be. You know, the ones wreaking havoc on society, fucking with politics and the economy, and generally doing things they aren't supposed to. There are more demons out there than just the ones trying to kill us. There are old-school ones who try to keep a low profile, helping their human capsules and making deals with the devil. I think we should jump on this. I mean, we *are* demon hunters, right?"

"You have intel?" Katie whispered, elbowing Stephanie.

"Yes," she replied. "But doofy over here won't listen to me."

'Hey, doofy!" Katie smirked. "Snap out of your trance and listen up! Girl has intel."

"*Thank* you." Stephanie smirked back.

"Okay." Korbin leaned forward. "And how exactly did you come by this intel? Can you trust the person who gave it to you? How do you know it's not a trap?"

"I can't tell you where I got it," she replied. "But you have trusted me with everything else, and I have the names of people who are actually infected. If *I* trust my source, you should too."

"These are the types of things we have to check out first." Korbin sighed. "We can't just roll into someone's home and take them down. What if they aren't demons? I mean, if the demon is staying on the down-low, the ring doesn't always show. If you go to one of these places, how are you going to be able to tell if the person has a demon or is just a really big asshole?"

"Uh, I think I can help with that." Katie raised her hand. "Pandora can give them the demon test before the person even knows we are there, so we will know. She is *that* good."

Pandora snickered. *Damn right.*

"See?" Stephanie pointed to her teammate. "I give you the names and locations, and then Wonder Girl over here can roll right up to the house and tell if they are human or not. If they aren't and they come to the door, we'll act like we are giving away bibles or something."

"Oh, yeah, that's rich." Korbin snorted. "The ex-madam and her superdemon sidekick posing as bible thumpers."

Katie and Stephanie just stared at him silently, no amusement on their faces. Korbin laughed, but slowly wiped the smile from his face. He took a deep breath and leaned back in his chair, rubbing his hands over his face.

"Ugh. You are putting me in a really tough position."

"Just let us try it. Let us prove to you that we don't have to wait for the demons to come to us," Stephanie argued. "We can catch them by surprise, and take care of it before anyone else knows. We will be taking care of the war on the outside and taking care of the underground on the back burner. Otherwise we win the war but we are still at war, only now they are masked."

"Fine." Korbin put up his hand before Stephanie could squeal with excitement. "You get one, and I mean *ONE*, trial run, so pick your best bet here."

"Yes, yes, yes," Stephanie chanted. "You are going to be ecstatic; beyond happy with the outcome, I promise you. Come on, Katie, let's go before he changes his mind."

The two girls ran out of the office, leaving Korbin kicking himself for giving in.

They headed up the stairs and jumped into Stephanie's

little red sports car. Katie smiled, remembering what it was like to have her own car.

Stephanie put the car in drive and zoomed down the road, heading toward the Strip. Katie leaned her head back and let the wind blow through her hair. The evening temperature was just perfect for a little excursion and some demon-killing.

The old man drove up his long driveway to the gate in the front of his house. He pressed the code in, and waited to pull his Bentley forward until it was all the way open. In front of him was a huge white house with perfect shrubbery and a perfect artificial lawn; the perfect place to come home to.

He was single and lived alone in the hills, working every day and then retiring to the scenic view of the lights of Vegas below him. He pulled his car into the garage and parked, opening the door and throwing his expensive designer suit jacket over his arm as he picked up his briefcase.

He clicked the button that shut the garage door and walked through the side entrance. He made his way through the dark house and went into his office down the hall. He yawned, dropping his briefcase on the floor and tossing his jacket on the chair. He turned to walk to his desk…and froze when he heard an unfamiliar voice.

"I know about you," the voice whispered. "How you use the *dark* forces, the demon inside you, to get ahead in life. I know about your deal with the devil, and I know how you treat others. Old man, you have finally met your truth."

The man turned right and left, feeling someone slither around him. At first he thought it was his imagination, his demon messing with him like he did sometimes, but when he called for him, he found him hiding inside, scared to death.

"Who's there?" he asked a bit louder. "I'll call the police!"

"And tell them what?" the voice hissed. "That your business has attracted too much attention and now people are starting to ask questions? That you have a demon in your head, and two in your home? That you are not what you seem? I don't think anyone can help you now, but then again you knew that already. What's the matter? You afraid to pay up on your debts?"

He shuddered. "Leave me alone."

The demonic voice terrified him even worse than the deal he had made with the devil.

It cut to his core. His demon continued to cower in the corner of his dark and ominous soul, begging for relief.

The man's hands shook wildly at his sides as he stared into a pair of bright-red eyes. He blinked, and they were gone. With a shaking hand he reached over and turned on the lamp, finding himself facing a white woman with dark hair pulled up in a knot, her eyes glowing red.

He panicked, yelling as he knocked the chair over behind him. He tried to work his way to the door.

Katie didn't move. She just tilted her head and looked at him with no expression.

He whimpered, then turned and made a run down the

dark hallway. As he reached the staircase a leg shot out from the right and slammed into his stomach, knocking him to all fours.

He groaned, holding his mid-section while trying to continue to crawl forward.

Tears streamed down his face as he cried out for help, but no one was there to hear him.

He collapsed onto the ground and laid there for a moment, and Stephanie stepped out of the shadows. Slowly he turned over on his back, his five-hundred-dollar tie sliding over his designer white shirt and flopping on the slick mahogany floor beneath him.

He choked and attempted to catch his breath, trying to stop himself from blubbering like an idiot.

Stephanie breathed in his horror, feeling every emotion he did. He didn't know who these women were, but he was certain his time was over. He was certain the devil had returned for his payment.

"Please," he whimpered. "I need more time; more time. It's not done yet."

Stephanie threw her head back and laughed, walking toward him in her red stilettos. She stopped next to him and pushed the toe of her shoe into his side.

She grimaced at even being that close to someone as despicable as him. She leaned over him and looked deep into his eyes, pursing her lips and then smiling coyly. He stopped crying and whimpered, waiting for her to speak.

"Rule Number One, *bitch*," Stephanie growled. "Always have backup!"

She punched him as hard as she could, knocking him unconscious.

This is my salutation and appreciation for not only reading through our story but also reading through our author notes as well!

"Welcome to the Jungle" is an interesting title. Part of it refers to the concrete jungle, and was inspired by the art which inspired our cover (a blown-up city block.)

Laurie asked me to come up with our next four titles and I was thinking DAMN!

No, really.

Now, I like dreaming up story titles, but for whatever reason I was running into a bit of a challenge figuring out the next four book titles so far in advance. However, she was pushing (I mean, "requesting") and what was I going to do but say "Yes, ma'am?" (Editor's Note: You find yourself in the position of saying that to a lot of your women, don't you, Michael?)

So, I have the cover concepts and I'm thinking "I want to *ROCK* this."

That got me thinking and the creative juices going, and we get *Welcome to the Jungle* (Book 05) for Guns N Roses... *Metal Up Your Ass* (Book 06) for Metallica, *Dirty Deeds Done Dirt Cheap* (thank you Pandora) by one of my favorite bands, AC/DC, and Metallica again with *For Whom the Bell Tolls* to finish out the arc.

Obviously these stories aren't based on the songs, but rather the intent of the story evokes (for me) the title of the book.

Expect a sword on the cover of book 06 for Metal Up Your Ass.

NEW SERIES...

So, I've been talking with Laurie about trying a spin-off of *Protected by the Damned*, but the plan was to create new characters (as discussed in previous *Author's Notes*) and see how the characters felt after we played with them in a story.

If I liked them, we would make plans to write a new series with them.

The dichotomy of the Odd Couple was on my mind as I conceived of Ella and Melnick—except this time Felix is the demon, and the teenage pain-in-the-ass is Oscar. Although Ella is perceiving opportunities in her life provided by Melnick, I have to believe she isn't done wanting her way.

Nor is Melnick finished explaining why Ella needs to do whatever-it-is his way.

Katie and Pandora are ass-kickers and door-breakers. I believe Ella and Melnick will be a bit more intelligent (eventually) about their solutions...but time will tell.

If you would like this series to go forward, I'd love to hear your 'Wahoo!' or something equivalent in the reviews on Amazon for this book OR in the Facebook group (we are almost five hundred strong now.)

THE FUTURE

These stories, and the support for these stories, has FAR exceeded our expectations! THANK YOU SO MUCH for purchasing them, reviewing them, and encouraging your friends who don't mind a little bit of a raunchy demon their literature to read them.

As always, if you *keep* supporting these stories, we will do our best to keep our wits about us and produce more of them to keep you chuckling or laughing out loud deep into the night. Although sometimes you might need to wipe a tear from your eye.

We have twelve (12) Katie and Pandora books planned. After that, who knows? I'm willing to consider how to expand the stories, and some ideas are starting to seep into my subconscious on just what needs to happen in book thirteen.

The world is going to get a bit bloodier before it gets better, but the ride will still be fun. I promise!

Ad Aeternitatem!

Michael Anderle

<*There, you punk-assed author, I wrote your fucking* Author Notes*! Now give me a fucking DONUT or I'll rip your balls off!*>

Can I just say to all the Axl Rose fans out there…the title of this book has me singing at the top of my lungs (inside my head). You too? Awesome. We should be friends.

It's been a few weeks. Feels like days over here in Psychoville. I would say it has a population of one, but I'm pretty sure Mister Anderle is the president/mayor/janitor.

I just fry up nuggets. Nothing to see here.

Don't read this if you have anything better to do. It's a bit rambly. It's 10pm, and I should have been asleep an hour ago. My sleep medication is causing rainbows to burst from my vision or something poetic like that.

It's been an interesting few weeks, and I'll tell you why.

We went up to Austin to look at land. Now we're in Houston, so this was a fun trip. I love Austin. The food is beyond outstanding, and there's plenty of it. I'm a foodie, and so is the hubs. We plan where we're going on vacation based on where the best restaurants are.

So we're looking for land, because my parents need their next thing. Mom is a retired pastor/church planter who gave up her retirement to serve in ministry most of her adult life. And my father was the manager of a mirror plant until he had a massive heart attack back in 2010 and his company of twenty-five years fired him.

Since then, he's been in a low-paying job that's a bit of a ministry too. When Hurricane Harvey came through here in Texas, it took their house and both of their cars. Needless to say it's been a rough few years, but here's the silver lining…we were in Austin looking for land for them.

We've been able to bring them on to work odd jobs with the publishing company I started three years ago, and pay them—not a ton, but enough to pay their bills—and give them a retirement on us. It's a blessing I've always wanted. It's not easy, but it's honestly beautiful.

And that's thanks to my fast fingers and you being willing to pick up a book. So thank you. I've thanked God for you guys, and all my readers everywhere multiple times in the last few weeks.

Because of all this tense madness, I decided a few days ago to start a new project...because doing ten thousand projects with Mike and a few other select people isn't enough on top of publishing the five to eight books that my brother or I write each month. (It's romance...not sure that's your cup of tea at all.) But this new project was for me.

You guys ever do that? Just decide enough is enough and you need something for yourself? That was this. No bubble bath, chocolates or massages here. No, sir. In Psychoville we have "me time" by writing sixty thousand more words a month.

I needed some old-fashioned humor. The seventy-year-old woman inside me was cracking too many jokes for me not to notice. Now, I'm forty, but I'm sure when I get to be seventy I'll be a mix of these two wise-cracking older ladies that I'm writing my first cozy mystery about.

I have a clip of it below. If you need a laugh, or like cozy mysteries at all—check it out. I told Mike I wanted to share what I'd been up to, and the best way to do that is just to drop some of the story. It's not much of it, but it felt damn good to get it out.

And I laughed until I had tears in my eyes. That's a good enough treat for me. Hope you enjoy it, and as always... thank you for all you do. I started writing to offer readers a bit of warmth, love, joy in their day, and I hope that's what we're still doing.

What I never expected was that my readers would help me take care of my folks. My appreciation is beyond words.

Slave to many stories,

Laurie Starkey

Excerpt from my not-yet-named Cozy Mystery:

(Forgive the editing mistakes. We don't edit until we're all done in my camp)

———

"I'm not sure why we torture ourselves week in and week out." Velma glanced at her sister-in-law, and Ethel let out a tight sigh. "We don't need a damn hobby. We've done all we should have! Our race is over. Give it a rest."

Without missing a beat, Ethel reached up and tuned the radio to some church music. "You obviously need a little Jesus in your day."

"Not this again." Ethel turned and let her eyes scan the mounds of bluebonnets they were driving by.

"You like to crochet. I know you do." Ethel was cut off by the car jerking. "You pretend with everyone else that you hate crafts, but you've been doing them for the better part of fifty years."

"It's better than killing folks and drinking myself into an early grave." Velma gripped the armrest on the door as the car lurched again. "When are you taking this piece of shit into the shop? If we got stuck on the side of the road, we'd end up having to walk a mile to get to the nearest station. That'd take all damn day with you and that bum hip you got."

"If we made it to the station," Ethel murmured under her breath, and pressed her foot to the gas. "You know these country people. We might end up in someone's supper."

Velma croaked out a laugh. "Someone's supper? Like in their stew?"

"Too hot for stew right now." Ethel reached over to play around with the air conditioner, only to get blasted in the face with hot air. "Jiminy Crickets."

Velma rolled down the window and shook her head. "No one is going to eat us." She glanced down and smirked. "Well, they might eat *me* cause I'm good eatin', but you? Not a chance."

"I'm ignoring that." Ethel turned the wheel and forced herself not to smile. They'd lived together for twenty-six years—since Alfred died—so she was more than used to Velma's quipping. She quite preferred it. Kept things interesting.

"Those two yellow lines are there for a reason." Velma unbuckled as the car stopped and turned toward Ethel, lifting an eyebrow for good measure. "Not worried about those buggers?"

"No clue what a bugger is." Ethel got out of the car, taking her time. The bum hip was no joke, especially when the Texas humidity hit in full force. "And don't be complaining about crochet class to me. You know it's all we have, other than each other. We're biding our time until we meet Jesus."

"And then the real party starts." Velma's gravelly voice carried over the car.

Ester let out a soft laugh, straightened her new frilly shirt, and moved to the back of the car to grab their stuff. "Come get your bag."

"Promise me that no matter what, you're not going to hate me today." Velma walked toward the trunk and waggled her eyebrows.

"Oh dear Lord. What did you do?" Ethel opened the trunk, pulled out both bags and handed Velma hers. Ethel's pink bag had crocheted flowers all over it; the little things were a pain in the ever-loving rear to get done.

Velma's was plain and black. "Like my soul," she'd muttered the last time Ethel had brought it up.

"I did what I was told to do." Velma took the bag, turned slowly, and walked toward the long strip center in front of them. "Just giving you a fair warning because we've been friends so long."

"Well, thank you...I think." Ethel moved up beside Velma, noticing that her friend had slowed down a little to wait on her. It was the little things in life that kept Ethel's spirits up. It had been a lonely life since Alfred had passed, but they were making do. Ethel knew that Velma missed her brother, but she never said a word. Typical Velma.

"I do miss the good old days. Teaching was a pain in my big jiggly ass, but it was something to do." Velma reached out and pulled open the door to the crochet class. "Now I spend my time tangled up in yarn and avoiding horny mailmen."

"Velma! Mr. Wallace is a nice guy. He's not..." Ethel struggled to say the word.

"Horny?" Velma asked as they walked in.

The pretty girl that instructed the class spat her coffee halfway across the room. "Ladies. Good to see you again!"

Velma snorted as Ethel gave her a stern look. "Please don't embarrass us today."

"I already did, apparently." Velma tugged her bag up on her shoulder and made her way across the room. A few familiar faces smiled her way, but she ignored them and plopped down in a chair just big enough for her. No need to make room for anyone else. Then she'd have to talk. Mingle. She shivered at the thought.

"Sorry about that." Ethel smiled at Nicole and reached out to cup the young woman's shoulder. "I love this shawl you're wearing. Did you make it yourself?"

Nicole glanced down and nodded. "I sure did. It's called the 'corner-to-corner' pattern. I'm thinking you probably know this one though, right, Ms. Ethel?" Her blue eyes rested on Ethel's face, and the warmth in her small smile made Ethel's lips lift too. The young woman was a joy, and kept the class laughing and fun.

"I remember trying to do this one as a girl, but it never turned out." Ethel released her and stepped back. "Where's Ray? He out today?"

"Right here, darlin'." Raymond Wetzel had been the hit of the high school in his younger days, but the poor old fellow thought he was still eighteen. "You need some Ray play?"

Nicole's eyes widened and she clapped her hands.

"Okay, class. On that note, let's get started. We have a lot to do today."

Ethel spun on her heel and shook her head. "You better behave, Mister. Jesus is watching you."

"He can take a few notes from this book." Ray tugged at his button-down shirt and bounced on the balls of his feet. The old guy had way too much vigor for his age.

"Blasphemy." Ethel let out a sigh, moved around him, and walked toward Velma. "Did you really sit in that single chair instead of the couch we usually share?"

"Yes," Velma barked. "Something's in the damn air around here. First ol' Calvin Wallace trying to strike up a conversation, and now Ray's swinging his—"

"Velma! Jeeze Louise!" Ethel took the seat next to her and pulled her bag into her lap. "Just don't talk unless someone talks to you."

"This seat taken?" Ray waggled his eyebrows and pointed to the seat on the other side of Velma.

"Yes, you gigolo." Velma dropped her bag into the chair and smirked. "Go spread your herpes somewhere else."

"Always feisty, Vel." He winked and turned his attention to Ethel. "You, on the other hand, are still just as pretty as you were the day we all graduated high school."

Ethel blushed. "Stop it, Ray. Go sit down somewhere. Nicole is trying to start the class."

Velma rolled her eyes, grabbed the walking stick that lay on the floor beside her, and whacked him in the knee with it. "Get on, now! Like a rabid dog."

"Damn, Velma. Why are you so violent, baby?" Ray tugged the stick from her hands.

"Mr. Wetzel? Time to find a chair, please. We're going

to get started on a new pattern here shortly." Nicole's sweet voice caused all three of them to stop.

"No problem, sugar plum." Ray glanced over his shoulder and winked at the young woman before giving Ethel a wink and Velma an eyebrow waggle. Silly biddies knew they all liked him. Well, there was enough to go around, for sure.

Velma grabbed the walking stick and shook it at him. "Get on down the road, Herp."

He chuckled and found a chair a little ways down.

"You know, you don't have to be so darned mean, Velma." Ethel took the stick from her and handed it to Nicole, who offered a hand to take it. "He's lonely like the rest of us."

"I'm not lonely, and he's hitting on everything that's got boobs in here." Velma reached over and grabbed her bag. "It ain't right, and you know it."

Ethel huffed and pulled out the blue and yellow bubble-pattern blanket she'd been working on. It reminded her of sunshine and freedom, because it was beautiful and bright.

"We're not dead yet, and I for one want to keep on living until I die." Ethel snorted and turned her attention to Nicole. She'd had more than enough of everyone. Slipping into the warmth of crafting was her great escape, and she did it as often as possible.

"All right, everyone." Nicole knelt in front of the half-circle of crocheters and pulled out a green blanket, then stood and lifted it. "This is what I did for my bubble pattern this last month. I know we were all working here and at home on our projects, but today is the day we're wrapping up this pattern and learning a new one. Anyone else want to share what they did?"

Crickets.

"Anyone?" Nicole looked around, hopeful. How people could be shy in their seventies was beyond her, but maybe it was a trait for all ages? Yes, that was definitely it.

"Oh, all right. I'll share." Ethel pulled the rest of her blanket out as her hands shook. "I made this one because it reminds me of my mother's kitchen when I was a girl. Daddy died when I was young and never got to live in the house, so after his passing my momma went into the new house and redecorated all of it. I think she did it to really figure out who she was without him. It was part of the healing process."

Ethel's eyes filled with tears. She reached up and brushed them away. The sniffles around the room surprised her.

"It's beautiful," Velma's voice was soft and her grip warm on Ethel's forearm. "She would have loved it."

"It is *gorgeous*, Ms. Ethel. Mind if I show everyone?" Nicole walked toward it and extended her hands. Her eyes were filled with tears.

"Sure, of course." Ethel handed it over and scooted her butt back in the chair, her back stiff. Everyone seemed to be having a moment over her confession, but that was all right. Life was precious, and remembering that was enough to take someone back a little.

"Crocheting isn't just about yarning over and picking your colors and making something beautiful." Nicole paused as she lifted the blanket up for everyone to see. "It's about finding yourself. Remembering and honoring, and like Ms. Ethel said—healing."

The group clapped, filling Ethel with a sense of pride.

"I love it. You did a great job." Nicole handed Ethel the blanket back. "Who else wants to share?"

"Velma?" Ethel glanced at her. "I know you've been working on something in that pretty gold yarn every night. You want to show it to us?"

"Nope." Velma released Ethel's arm and pulled her bag close to her, hugging it like it was full of hundred-dollar bills.

"What? Why?" Ethel shifted in her chair a little.

"That's all right. Someone else, maybe?" Nicole turned to the rest of the group.

One by one, each person shared their blankets, bonnets, and shawls in the bubble pattern Nicole had taught them a month earlier. Ray's half-done baby blanket caused everyone to chuckle, but the old man seemed to enjoy the laughter more than the praise everyone else was after.

"Velma? Last chance." Nicole smiled and put her hands on her hips. "You know you're the best crafter in here. Whether you like it or not, your attention to detail is just fantastic."

"Velma. Show the woman what you did with her teaching. Good grief and gravy." Ethel sighed and tugged at Velma's bag.

"All right. Dammit to hell." She tugged the bag back and rolled her eyes. "Promise not to hate me?"

Ethel's stomach tightened. "Oh Lord. Maybe it's better if you don't—"

"I made something practical. I have twenty damn blankets around the house, and if none of y'all have noticed, it's hotter than Satan's crotch here. We live in *Texas*. Ain't nobody in their right mind wrapping up in a blanket." Velma pulled out the item she'd been working on and held it up. "I'm sending these to my cousin Belinda up in Maine. I'm pretty sure she needs them more than I do."

Nicole pressed her hand to her mouth as her eyes widened. Surely not.

"Are those panties?" Ray's voice was pitched higher than usual.

"Damn straight, and I made them big enough to fit over Belinda's Depends. She ain't young like us." Velma winked at Ethel. "You think she'll like them?"

"You're going to hell," Ethel whispered before cracking up.

"And on that note," Nicole whispered roughly, "get out your needles and some new yarn. We're learning a new pattern today, which is the one I used on my shawl. It's called 'corner-to-corner.'"

Hope you enjoyed it. Appreciate you beyond what you can understand.

Laurie aka Lulu Baxter for the project above.

PROTECTED BY THE DAMNED

THE BORIS CHRONICLES

with Paul C. Middleton

<u>Evacuation</u> (01) - Retaliation (02) - Revelations (03) - Redemption (04)

RECLAIMING HONOR

with Justin Sloan

<u>Justice Is Calling</u> (01) - Claimed By Honor (02) - Judgement Has Fallen (03) - Angel of Reckoning (04) - Born Into Flames (05) - Defending The Lost (06) - Saved By Valor (07) - Return of Victory (08)

THE ETHERIC ACADEMY

with TS Paul

<u>ALPHA CLASS</u> (01) - ALPHA CLASS: Engineering (02)

with N.D. Roberts

Discovery (03)

TERRY HENRY "TH" WALTON CHRONICLES

with Craig Martelle

<u>Nomad Found</u> (01) - Nomad Redeemed (02) - Nomad Unleashed (03) - Nomad Supreme (04) - Nomad's Fury (05) - Nomad's Justice (06) - Nomad Avenged (07) - Nomad Mortis (08) - Nomad's Force (09) - Nomad's Galaxy (10)

TRIALS AND TRIBULATIONS

with Natalie Grey

<u>Risk Be Damned</u> (01) - Damned to Hell (02)

~THE AGE OF MAGIC~

THE RISE OF MAGIC

with CM Raymond and LE Barbant

<u>Restriction</u> (01) - Reawakening (02) - Rebellion (03) - Revolution (04) - Unlawful Passage (05) - Darkness Rises (06) - The Gods Beneath (07) - Reborn (08)

THE HIDDEN MAGIC CHRONICLES

with Justin Sloan

<u>Shades of Light</u> (01) - Shades of Dark (02) - Shades of Glory (03) - Shades of Justice (04)

STORMS OF MAGIC

with PT Hylton

<u>Storm Raiders</u> (01) - Storm Callers (02) - Storm Breakers (03) - Storm Warrior (04)

TALES OF THE FEISTY DRUID

with Candy Crum

<u>The Arcadian Druid</u> (01) - The Undying Illusionist (02) - The Frozen Wasteland (03) - The Deceiver (04) - The Lost (05) - The Damned (06) - Into The Maelstrom (07)

PATH OF HEROES

with Brandon Barr

<u>Rogue Mage</u> (01)

A NEW DAWN

with Amy Hopkins

<u>Dawn of Destiny</u> (01) - Dawn of Darkness (02) - Dawn of Deliverance (03) - Dawn of Days (04) - Broken Skies (05)

TALES OF THE WELLSPRING KNIGHT

with P.J. Cherubino

<u>Knight's Creed</u> (01) - Knight's Struggle (02)

~THE AGE OF MADNESS~

LIVE FREE OR DIE

with Haley Lawson

Unleashing Madness (01)

~THE AGE OF EXPANSION~

THE ASCENSION MYTH

*with Ell Leigh Clarke *

<u>Awakened</u> (01) - Activated (02) - Called (03) - Sanctioned (04) - Rebirth (05) - Retribution (06) - Cloaked (07) - Bourne (08) - Committed (09)

CONFESSIONS OF A SPACE ANTHROPOLOGIST

with Ell Leigh Clarke

<u>Giles Kurns: Rogue Operator</u> (01) - Giles Kurns: Rogue Instigator (02)

THE UPRISE SAGA

*with Amy Duboff *

Covert Talents (01) - Endless Advance (02) - Veiled Designs (03) -
Dark Rivals (04)

BAD COMPANY

with Craig Martelle

The Bad Company (01) - Blockade (02) - Price of Freedom (03)

THE GHOST SQUADRON

with Sarah Noffke

Formation (01) - Exploration (02) - Evolution (03) -
Degeneration (04) - Impersonation (05) - Recollection (06)

VALERIE'S ELITES

with Justin Sloan and PT Hylton

Valerie's Elites (01) - Death Defied (02) - Prime Enforcer (03)
Justice Earned (04)

SHADOW VANGUARD

with Tom Dublin

Gravity Storm (01)

ETHERIC ADVENTURES: ANNE AND JINX

with S.R. Russell

Etheric Recruit (01) - Etheric Researcher (02)

Other Books

with Craig Martelle & Justin Sloan

Gateway to the Universe

~THE REVELATIONS OF ORICERAN~

THE LEIRA CHRONICLES

with Martha Carr

Waking Magic (01) - Release of Magic (02) - Protection of Magic (03) - Rule of Magic (04) - Dealing in Magic (05) - Theft of Magic (06) - Enemies of Magic (07) - Guardians of Magic (08)

SHORT STORIES

You Don't Touch John's Cousin: Frank Kurns Stories of the UnknownWorld 01 (7.5)

Bitch's Night Out: Frank Kurns Stories of the UnknownWorld 02 (9.5)

with Natalie Grey

Bellatrix: Frank Kurns Stories of the Unknownworld 03 (13.25)

Challenges: Frank Kurns Stories of the Unknownworld 04

AudioBooks

Available at Audible.com and iTunes

CLICK HERE TO SEE ALL LMBPN BOOKS ON AUDIBLE